D1431108

This Our Exile
Short Stories

Joshua Hren

This Our Exile
Short Stories

Angelico Press

First published in the USA and UK
by Angelico Press
© Joshua Hren 2017

All rights reserved

No part of this book may be reproduced or transmitted,
in any form or by any means, without permission

For information, address:
Angelico Press
169 Monitor St.
Brooklyn, NY 11222
angelicopress.com

ISBN 978-1-62138-321-5 (pb)
ISBN 978-1-62138-322-2 (cloth)
ISBN 978-1-62138-323-9 (ebook)

Cover Image:
"Ruine der Frauenkirche gegen Rathausturm,"
circa 1965, Richard Peter (1895–1977)
Cover Design: Michael Schrauzer

CONTENTS

Acknowledgments

"Wrecking Ball" originally appeared as "Editor's Choice" in *Relief*

"Control" originally appeared in *Relief*

"Sacré Cœur" originally appeared in *Dappled Things* Literary Journal, under the pseudonym Micah Cawber. The story was nominated for a Pushcart Prize.

"Heavyweight" originally appeared in *Aethlon* Literary Journal

"Copper" originally appeared in *Ink and Letters*

"In a Better Place" originally appeared in *Windhover*

"The Man Watching" originally appeared in *Windhover*

"Gates of Eden" originally appeared in *Windhover*

"Everything Must Go" earned Top-25 in *Glimmer Train's* 2009 Fiction Open

"Concluding Unscientific Postscript" was a finalist in the 2016 Fish Publishing Flash Fiction Contest

For my wife—
who has been,
is,
and will be
there.

Man has places in his heart which do not yet exist,
and into them enters suffering,
in order that they may have existence.
Léon Bloy

Daedalus interea Creten longumque perosus
exilium tactusque loci natalis amore
—Ovid, *Metamorphoses*

Wrecking Ball

How I came to it I cannot rightly say,
So drugged and loose with sleep I had become
When I first wandered there from the true way
Dante, *The Inferno*

BLAISE STOOD AT THE BASE of the abandoned brewery, his bicycle stretched across his back like a stiff casualty. His father had worked here until his middle-aged death. If fifty is the middle. Blaise had not intended to pass this way, but some sharp street-scrap had punctured his tire and, indirectly, sent him into a long-forgotten section of the city. Normally, after a night of drinks with friends, he would cycle the three miles of well-lighted streets from Homer's Tavern home. To Sophia. Sophia, who without waking would leave a kiss on his cold cheek. And he would sleep.

But this night all pleasant rituals had met interruption. He had stayed late. He had told a small crowd of passively disapproving eyes that his wife was pregnant. He said it with a massive grin: "Sophia. She's a, is. With child. Our child." The conversation, for once, heated beyond lukewarm. He rubbed his collar bone as he found himself listening to hot, spitty talk of overpopulation and secret knowledge of financial packages likely to garner the interest now necessary for the future. The conversation swirled with its own life, around him, almost without him. Friends used the words "well-being" and "unhealthy" at least five times respectively. Then Brian J. asked him if he planned at last to get a job, a real job, and quit the dream life—whatever scribbles he was wasting ink on behind the E.R. welcome desk. These days the scribbles were turning into caricatures of the likes of Brian, business types who managed to stay hip. And it was then, as he reached into his back pocket and crumpled in seven seconds a run of sketches that had taken him seventy hours to complete, that most around the table rose to move on to another bar or to their beckoning homes. He looked sourly at the blinking lights forming untranslatable codes on the marble table, heard for the first time the solitary jazz encircling him, knowing that surely some friends somewhere knew some part of the truth about one another, but doubting whether he could handle it if they did. Swallowing the last of his tall black ale, he got up to go.

Margaret, closing in on the bottom of her fourth Manhattan, turned around, held his wrist and whispered, "You two'll be fine. Say I send congratulations," and she promised to knit a neutral-colored hat fit for a newborn.

The confluence of disapprovals made him slow. And, to slow him down further, after a few blocks of angry pedaling came the puncture, and he had to walk. His cell phone was waiting for him, suckling electricity as it slept at home, nestled in its crib. Instead of worrying over whether his wife was concerned over his where-abouts, he found himself wrestling with something coming into definition, something supremely lofty and supremely of the earth. Pursuing what he first swore was a vaguely-remembered short cut, he soured as the street names lost significance, then slowed in a stupor as he found himself small before the ruins of the old Brewer beer grounds. Stared at by the ruins of the old Brewer beer grounds, the blocks and blocks of mostly whole but dormant buildings with their dusky yellow windows serving as the stained-glass of the industrial age. He set down his bike, almost in awe of these shrines to gods now dead. As he shattered an already neck-less golden-brown bottle against a wall, Blaise was pulled back to the days when piles of shattered glass substituted for gold in the imagined worlds he and his childhood friends inhabited. Although, two weeks after finding out he was a father for the first time, he still clung to the plot which he had given to his life. He found himself, despite one extra beer per night at Homer's Tavern, stupefied by the little cell Sophia's body bore, shaking his head, sometimes, as though this ought not to have happened to him, to her. Sweeping the floor longer, so that the corn fiber bristles broke off, and he had to sweep the broom itself. Waiting until he heard heavy breathing, and then folding into bed. Pretending no life hid inside her as he traced the freckles on her neck. And wondering how much of his story he had ever truly told.

Blaise confronted the cream-brick building as though he and it were caught in an old, recurring argument, then backed away. The cream was mostly charred, but in spots you could see the simple, humble, yellow-white of yesterday. The very foundations yearned to be made living, to be clicking, stamping, busy with productivity. Barely ascertainable mementos of barley and hops, the scent constantly stuck to Pop's work shirt, met Blaise's nose and, led him to trespass inside. It was the same scent that Blaise had smelled when, leaning into the funeral casket, he saw with relief that, under the foundation makeup, his father's finger nails were black with irrevocable grease.

Blaise was suddenly glad his tire had popped as he felt the electric fuzz of anxiety fade in the face of this garden of mastered metals. These, with the accompaniment of a few men clocking in and out and in and out for a few decades, had made the city of Mill, had made the dollars that bought the brick and steel that Mill was made of. And, over time, the place had claimed his father's life, making him some kind of unknown and unknowing martyr. Looking at the rusty buildings was like looking at a slow torture chamber from that angle. He looked away, then back again.

The overgrowth of orphaned tools poised around him, insisting they still had power, assumed an overgrown purpose: they wanted to bottle him, send him like a message into the past.

Blaise looked at his clean hands. Bottle after bottle of jobs for bottle-necked men bending over for them, matching blue shoulders: a civilian army. Dad, giving the place everything he had, making it to manager of the brewery hands, handing them paychecks and dismissals, pulling the cord that made the whistle creak, then stopping at St. Joseph's for daily Mass before heading home. Blaise folded his hands, wondering what his father had seen and done day after day in that poorly lit Gothic church he had dismissed by fourteen. Is that where he went to cry? Blaise could see him kneeling there, eyes pressed against a bicep, being weak in a way he never was at home. Muttering little flickers of worry. Alongside those votive candles. Tonguing things to God.

This was all too much—thrilling and threatening at once. Like the time when his grandfather and father and the feeling of forever sat him down and structured him, instructed that he, too, would come to this temple of bottled spirits to put in his dues. The plant had closed instead, had freed Blaise. But what did it free him from? It wouldn't have been so bad. That—the menial job, the inescapable mundane—was, is, the lot of life. And the perfecting of sketches was so much the same: draft after draft and all the while wondering what would still be there though the inspiration had gone. A good enough job, decent enough benefits. As grandpa said, the shoe fits.

Grandfather. Father. In his mind Blaise fell back to that day with increasing momentum, but he was also here, now. They did not need to take him into this place to prove their points. They did not need to dirty his hands—only to show him theirs. They sat him down and looked at one another with a single look that said: he'll understand. And then they said things straight. When he was able even to get close, he could only come back to the memory in black and white: his father facing him without too much feeling, with hands folded as though praying to find words for the story told and retold—the this is your lot in life, son—and all the while he examined Blaise through coke-bottle glasses, the glare blaring, he not caring but for his wife, family, stability. Everything else was flowery, was futility.

Grasping a rusted handle, Blaise gasped and ambled into the headquarters of the bottling room with its empty bar of workers' stools. He was good as gold, his old man. Groveling here, too many years after the *this is your lot,* Blaise was sold. A good enough job. Decent enough benefits. The shoes shined, the outfit. Blue and common and enough. He saw the brewer's shirt now, faded in the dim, and, touching it, felt the way somebody's sweat had left the collar stiff. It should have been his neck here, sweating. Father. Grandfather. They should have taken him here after all. Then their points would not have needed proving. It hung on a hook on the otherwise empty wall of the factory as long as a football field. He was here, but felt as thin as the hung shirt, as though his full body were there. Stood below the blue shirt and trousers as though they were his very father, thin as a ghost but there. How to ransom the time. Stripping quickly in the cold, he put the clothes on and went back fully into Grandpa's living room, that room so many years ago, ready to understand.

"BLAISE, a time comes when, well, them thoughts, stories..." cringing trying to compete with the glory of the fairy tales, the fictions, anything untrue put down on paper or in the mind. His father coughed. "Your mother fed you them when you were small enough to take 'em seriously, but them stories gotta go. You gotta grow up, give in. Take it from these eyes." He could sense his own failure to see what they were seeing, but he smiled. Stupidly. Grandpa nodded, his neck veins violet, the color of bruises and imperial orchids.

Blaise hid his hands in his back pocket, crumpled there a cartoon to be sent out for publication. "I got a job at Maxwell's Meat's, Dad. Been workin' there going on three years now." A good enough job. Decent enough, bereft of financial fits.

"*Meats.* You—you just can't compete in that. In this world. Listen," a grave secrecy was sworn between them, signed by a look he'd learned to read, "sooner than later you gonna get tired of cleaning meats. You're gonna get lost in some gal and get this thrill, this crazy, I mean it might as well be like someone just wired you with an electric current or something, and you're gonna say to yourself, if you don't say it out loud, 'I need a good job, with decent benefits.' That's Brewer. A good job. Decent enough benefits. The shoe fits." He lifted the heel of his foot and Blaise, nineteen, drew a new caricature cartoon in his mind. Balked.

A good rob. Decent enough derelicts. The shoe's sole stinks like shit.

Now, then, the rest of the room came into focus. His father stepped back, seemed to center himself in the orange and yellow living room with yellow couches and tangerine tabletop, though the sun never danced, never dared its way through the thick marmalade curtains curtailing the light. Drapes doubled over the curtains, denouncing any foreign brightness but that emitting from each of the four corners of the common room. His father had finished pacing and was standing under the most powerful, central fluorescent, here, where the dreamy dawn never dared to poke its rosy fingers. Here where they had made their own center, had sunk the sun into the furniture, their faces felt large as planets. They faced him. The younger of the elders said, "There's no future as an artist. Which is what you been doing, what's making you lag and lean on Meats." He said this apocalyptically, as if to say, "There's no future."

Maybe because they could stand there, irises ridden with fifty and twenty-five years past the date of Blaise's dabble with the meat trade, past their own now buried prophecies of nineteen, before their own problems with coronary artery and prostate and spleen, before their marriages to sober wives and spendthrift practicality. And he, not even twenty, needed to see.

AND now, ready to resign to the factory line, to let loose his dogmatic cling to all art-aspirations, even the compromise that had been his stint with cartoons, the place is not ready for him, is halfway to becoming a museum.

She is pregnant. The thought permeated him more powerfully than the black ale still making its way out of his system. He waded into a conjured delivery room still nine months away, when he would be twenty nine, and, surpassing the here and now for Sophia's purple face and the face their one flesh had made, he cast his bets, and, yes, *a good enough job, decent enough benefits.*

BUT then again Blaise wanted to be back. To more than remember. And, changing history for the first time, in the center of the stuffy room, he ripped apart the marmalade curtains and grandfather first grabbed his handkerchief and covered but thought better and tilted his head back, squinting and smacked by the light.

"Not in my house," grandfather said with mustered anger. But the meat of it was melancholic. The anger was the bitterly spiced mustard. The old man's hearing aids chirped as he lunged forward, fell sideways slowly. Blaise disbelieved but, stuck under the past he had trespassed into, he closed the curtains quickly. Cut the light. No matter. He was dead. Grandpa. And, as they say, in a way, Papa. Pop.

HERE, in the brewery graveyard, Blaise was deadly young again and, trembling from cold inside, he looked outward, forward, for something worth living for, pouring over the brewery, the empty barley bags padding the walls of his future fifty-hour-a-week home. The bones of the factory would live again. He would work. A real job. He was alone. Leaning on the darkened door of the elevated office, his father's precipice, he pulled the whistle rope and hung his right hand, wrapping it so tight that when the whistle went off his knuckles went blue.

A good enough sob. Decent enough memory fits. His shoes didn't fit.

Snow had sneaked in and, long ago melted, now surfaced as ice under his feet. Cold feet. A father in his father's blue uniform.

After the whistle let out a delayed shriek he found out how strong the garden of metals and tools, in their silence, could be. Then a blanket, taken until now for a tarp, lumped to and fro, below him. Above, anything but idle, all his muscles made the same strain. Fear. "Who's here?" he clamored to clear the air.

The tarp, looking again like an empty barley bag, coarse and grainy, gained focus under the pack of matches from Homer's, which still sold bottles of beer once made here; he set off all thirty heads at once blazing against the translucent dark beyond midnight.

Blaise leaped toward the tossing worming sack and, faithful, his feet landed him upright, if even still on ice. He poked the balled up man with the tip of his boot. A human, a mangled man. A hair-covered ear emerged first, toes rustling, heels kicking at the other end. Near the head of the wormy man's soft shell, a cut-wired circuit box read, in red ink that bled so that he could hardly read the words, "Out of Order: Do Not Use." There was no way the last buzz of the black ale could conjure this. Blaise backed away, but he couldn't go back to his grandfather's living room. Some scratchy thought in his head said *don't look back,* again and again like a Bob Dylan record stuck on repeat.

The head, wet with warmth, steamed faintly. Whispers of *am I dreaming* rose with the heat. The homeless man said, "In this two thousand and eighth year of our Lord, I live if for no other reason to give a licking to all who pass me by, by and by and by," with fierce, wide awake focus.

Blaise browsed the contents of the sleeping sack, which was slit down the center. At least sixteen newspaper pages lined the length of the eye-rubbing man, some inside his clothes like insulation and some outside, like worn advertisements. Other contents: two bread loaves, a liter of bottled water, pocket sized Bible bent in a rainbow arch, a pack of Black and Milds cigarillos. As if awaking a second time, the man shot up, his body in a capital *L*, and then the light left for good, the rosy-fingered flames from

Homer's going marmalade before burning out. Blaise backed off, felt for his keys, wallet. Checked quickly if his shoes were tied.

The scowl-faced man said, "I get so nerve—get so nervous now, everyday now, everyday. Stay, lay down here, son, here my laudable professor: tell me why I lost her. Professor. Smart I see. Saw."

"He's blessed. We blessed." Another voice, vintage, rich with drink, entered from the other side of the circuit box. No face, just, "Hawthorne get outta prison yesterday, for forty years. I've been there too, but for less. We been walking, free, *free*, been making our way to Chicago—work there. Thought I'd set up shop, since I'm in the city. You can read?" A paper touched Blaise's palm before he recognized another man inches from his face, toe to toe. The light from outside was almost dead by the time it reached here.

"Got this from the humanservices. Gotdamn the *human* services, sons of guns gimme it and send me off and who am I to say then, 'I can't read,' since I been in jail so long, not just, not that I couldn't of figured it out in there but what was the point tell me what was the point?" The first man, his sack shed completely, sprawled on the earth like the skin of a bean, slapped his thigh and said, "Not just that he's stupid. He been in solitary *refinement*. Didn't care to read and write no more in there."

"—Can talk for myself, Hawthorne. Been talked for and talked at for ten years, and it's mine to start opening my own mouth." Blaise did not blink at them. The brewery, the one he was to work in, the benefits and the shoes that fit—it was gone. It was now a house and home decorated by the prison-made. He backed away again. Bit by bit, maybe, he could get out.

"Still, it's not that freedom comes and then you use it till it gets taken away again," one of them said in a mock-serious social worker and wisdom wringer voice. It was hard to strain the eyes and see. Then a train, behind the brewery, and a great noise and light.

Hawthorne finalized his stance. Completely vertical he was

less intimidating: medium height, meager in muscle. "Neither us need a nanny now. Leave that to the State, hey Pastor?" Pastor pulled back his paper, perhaps aware that foreign street lamps held no match to the matchless grayness of the brewery grave-yard. Nothing could be read, really, words or faces or traces of the times when work was where they were: the whistle pull had shorted out an off-and-on-again light living in the lot outside, turning everything unreal as twilight. But the bruise on the bottom of Blaise's heel hurt, so he knew he was still standing on solid ground. "I can't get my check till this paperwork gets through. Gotta sit for four hours in the stink of lazy ladies and a bunch of bottom feeders."

Hawthorne smiled, hunched toward Blaise, held out a question like a knife. "You haven't the slightest idea what Pastor did time for, do ya?" He grew, lost it, grew again into a smile that both comforted and caused suspicion, stoking the sense that this was unreal. "His daughter died. And he killed her—or so they, so they said—then they messed, missed with him, cause he prayed. That's right, jailed for praying. A modern day martyr. Said he should've taken his daughter to the doctors. Handed her over to them…huh. Said he knew she had an illness, had an illness born of the body not the soul, and ain't no praying gonna sow it up. Sure enough easy to do that—but Pastor—ain't that right?"

Blaise couldn't be sure but the chiseled caves around Pastor's eyes glistened with what must have been the holy water of the broken. "Ain't that right. Pastor was not among the unrighteous, he was godly in all his days at work, Security Guard for seventeen years at Saley's. Was godly at the setting sun, too, tucking his Tamara into bed at night and praying, laying hands over her head to keep the demons down, to cut the thorn of Satan from the flesh of his favorite girl. Sometimes, when she get sweaty, he stays up till all hours, four, five, all night, fighting the hot of her skin with his faith. But he—," but he broke it off when Pastor slipped his belt off and beat the buckle against the Out of Order sign, shouting, "But I failed, my faith failed me! My doubt, what can a man say? It got me jailed."

"Martyr." Hawthorne said it humbly, as though his mind was lined with whiskey, hyper-aware of his homelessness in a world whose masters had lorded it over his friend here.

"Don't, damn it, don't pedestal me, please," Pastor pleaded. "Ain't no glory outside a God, and God gone from this here earth."

"In this year of our Lord, two thousand and eight." Hawthorne hurriedly brought the conversation to a circle, but it was really like an oval, like a blind eye seeing a blotch of ink black, a splotch seen constant and clear, traces of twilight twinning on the sides, waiting, not pushing into the inkwell, swelling, so that they engulfed it whole, but still none of the three seemed to see. The unintelligent design of the eye. "Ain't nobody less here than He."

Blaise blinked. He had to be back at work in a few hours. The early shift, behind the desk in the emergency room. A part time gig. It had to go. No real benefits. A decent job. Oh shit. When he reached into his very heart, though, and felt around for the love or even the nerve he needed to put off his plots and get a godforsaken job, he found not more than a few drops of blood ready for the shedding. And he couldn't dole it out like dishwater.

"The end is near," Pastor dutifully denounced, and at once but this time only for a moment Blaise saw the marmalade curtains, saw his father's and grandfather's faces rotating like discontent planets. Pastor went on. "Don't be left, don't be left here, this earth, son—take it from someone who knows: The good God ain't here no more. He left when Jesus went back up into the heaven, and if he ever comes down it's not for you and me."

Blaise, sitting on the shoulders of his father, in the past, in this very brewery, remembered the ration of good his father had seen in him, a ration that had lasted until today, and asked, "Pastor, um, sorry—I don't mean to argue or," he backed away a bit, "but what about goodness? I mean God created the world and looked upon it and called it good. That's what they told me He did. And all that?" Blaise remembered, once, his father saying to his mother something about goodness and sinners, God not bent on the righteous, something he heard at Mass: the difference between being righteous and virtuous, but he could not make meanings from this memory. He looked at himself in Pastor's eye, in a flick of light thrown down by the passing train.

Generically, Pastor, as if reading from a cheat sheet, said, "Man has fallen. The apple. The garden—you know it. The world is gone under the reign of the ruler of lies. Nobody but a fool could believe else-wise. I was born under a sign that said so, so I didn't need to learn it to trust it: father was fitn' to get outta jail the week after I was born, and, I guess he did, long enough to take the train back and find me swathed in some headscarves passed down by momma's sisters and grandmothers, and all, so that my dad says, 'Gonna make him a man by dressing him prissy,' and, so my momma retold me many times over, he scooped me up by the hands and dangled me naked, saying, 'naked we came into this world, and naked we gonna leave it.' Fathers. They know damn good how to put the fear of life into you. God." Light burgled itself into the brewery.

"Jesus," said Pastor, and he spat like it was a prayer.

Back to his father's daily visits to St. Joseph's, to the vigil flicks and their mute prayers, Blaise could not help wincing when he heard the name *Jesus*. Hawthorne hung on Pastor's arm, started departing and dragging him with, settling the silly hopes he was holding about the lost young man learning the light of life. As a finale Pastor, pulled out the dock door, said, "Remember. One bridge. Only one." Then, "Maybe I'm wrong," but by the time Blaise asked, "Wrong about what?" they were gone, and in the dark distance they looked to him like two stepping stones, rolling. If they were real it was their overwhelming aura of absurdity that worked on him the hardest.

Blaise rushed to sort some outline of sanity, some *why* out of the resuscitated men. He dug his hands into the earth on which they had closed their eyes, but the sackcloth was ashes, or something ashy was spread across the place where it had been. An old fire pit? The resuscitated men took their sackcloth with them. Nothing was left of the godly. Just the good that God and his father had made. He was once good. Here. Blaise felt awful. Off balance, he leaned against the wall. The entire talk with his father and grandfather, with Pastor and Hawthorne sat uneasy, like undercooked eggs that had wanted badly to be chickens before the life got chilled out of them.

Pastor was full. Of pathology, sure, but also something stronger, something Blaise closed his eyes to see, clearly, in the dark. There was no kindness you could count on in man. But—he came to the bridge—but they had burned it, belted out the backdoor, beyond the conveyor belt, left only a sweltering sting. He knew it well, felt his face swell the way he had seen it on so many faces of so many souls with whom he had burned bridges and bolted. Lightning. He felt as though he had half of something. But he did not know what the other half was. Good. God.

He was done going to Homer's. He would not be burning any bridges. They were more filler than friends. Somehow he had capably burnt bridges between himself and as many actual friends as he could count on ten fingers, but only the bridge was burned, not the pile of persons, who were still somewhere. Broken bicycle led him to walk home. Walk home made him stop here. Serendipity. Bullshit. His mind whirred with the echo of the faraway train, programmed never to intersect with another. The train bridge. Ten years old. He ran across it on a dare. His friends ran the other way, afraid of death or heroic deeds. Which? Burning bridges did not block them from coming back. It just meant that every time he talked to them he did so from a charred precipice, a pulpit from which he was always shouting, though the words came out so shyly they barely showed themselves.

And then their souls would sneak up from some other side anyhow. "I'm done being done. Ready. I *remember*," he yelled into the space between the Pastor and his mouth, swiveling to the south where, dock door left open, a pall of fresh snowflakes was finding its place atop the foundation of his family, the city—the brewery. In the sky shone the first peek of the gold, dying future, and also the brilliant glistening of the marmalade curtains of the past. The sun, the sun. Nothing new. The same old sun. He pushed against the brewery wall, wrestling not with an angel but a monument of the meanness to come, of which his father had warned in sum: *a good enough job. Decent enough benefits. The shoe fits.* He managed to make out quarter to three on the digital clock tower down the street.

Sophia was pregnant. There was nothing past about it. He put this thought on, like a coat of arms. This was not a concept. It was a conception: she had conceived. The night, the morning, wherever he was it was immaculate. Impeccable flecks of fragile white falling, coloring his hair as if with the wash of worry. Snow was sperm, permanently altering the egg of the earth and the globe of his mind. He pushed at the brewery wall with all his might, and, tendons tight, fell for all that before it. But not in worship, not in fear and trembling. In steady, sober acceptance of unknowing that stopped short of the cynical snarl-smile that so often found its way onto his face.

Then, kneeling, he saw, rusted, the raised boom and dangling wrecking ball, impotent, poised to destroy but without the fore-shadowing it once would have carried. It had been abandoned with the brewery. Climbing the operator's orange ladder, pressing his cold palms against the colder metal, he mounted the metallic beast as, in myths, heroes sit astride great birds of fortune. He could not have been more than twenty feet above the earth, but this height made him feel drunk, as though the brew of time past and the fermentation of the future had made its way into his body. If she was, he was pregnant too, with something which he did not know yet. Something that was making all things new. Factories rise and fall. Specializations become spent: this factory would never make good on the things it was made for again. He gripped one of the levers to his right, purposefully, and the snow melted against his hand. He sniffled. Itching to move, to gain warmth, he found his body without premeditation crawling across the boom as, in childhood, he had inched across great tree branches. From the tip he fell down around the chain, his hands and crotch burning by the time he reached the wrecking ball.

Swinging it, he asked it to do what it could not do. He asked it to do that kind of creation which can only be destruction. He begged it to wreck the things in his foundations that stood no chance and leave the parts from which, in the coming months of salvage when he would have to seek scraps in himself not obsolete, he would forge what could be called good. He teetered, making the ball move. Finally, like a five-year-old boy who, pumping his legs, makes the swing rush beyond his control, Blaise watched himself, flung by the wrecking ball, to the earth. It was only then, when his ankles sprained and shooting pains overwhelmed his nerves, that, groping after the chimera of the individual whom he once knew himself to be, to become, he did not find it. He was hungry. But his eyes did the salivating; his mouth stayed dry. Blaise's whetted vision blurred all the city's faraway lights into a single glow that shone with more than the sum of its parts.

Sacré Cœur

DALTON SQUEEZED the bulb baster and watched the bacon grease rise slowly, like cholesterol plaque, into its plastic heart. His own heart palpitated, pausing and pounding erratically, as it had come to do lately. Inhaling deeply and flexing his lungs loudly, he managed a few small steps that led him to the window and he stuck his head out to be sure neither children nor solicitors were leaning against the apartment's brick base. Satisfied, he let the grease splatter on the yellow and red petunias three floors below. Most blooms caught the substance with resilience, but the weaker ones withered immediately, collapsing like soldiers under chemical agents. Over the rising stove-top sizzle Dalton heard Marie scratching her skin in the next room. She sounded like a dog, fresh from the fields, raking off the day's parasites. He waited for her scold, but perhaps she had not heard the grease drop. Marie preferred that he use the bulb baster to slurp up the bacon grease and then proceed to drip it back over the meat, for flavor. Or at least she used to. His shoulders, which were almost up to his ears, relaxed as he remembered her strange new turn. She probably would not even mind that he cut off the white parts of the raw bacon, unable in good conscience to feed another human soul such outright fat after his last doctor visit and the precautions he had been told he must now take. Not that Marie was overweight. In fact, the strange new turn had taken a good twenty pounds from her already thin frame. *I bet,* he teased her interiorly, laughed to himself, turning the bacon again, letting one side go crisp, the way she liked it, *I bet it'd make her happy if I burnt the whole batch.* And he imagined his hand, gloved in white muslin, lifting a silver, half-sphere plate covering—something like the top of a government building or a basilica—and presenting her the twisted black writhes of bacon.

Marie was Dalton's daughter, but he only saw her once a week, Saturday afternoon through Sunday afternoon. She came by bus from Ozauk, three counties away, where she stayed with her mother, Glenda Ames, who, once his wife, had switched back to her maiden name. Preferred Glenda Ames to Glenda Shifler aesthetically anyhow. Dalton lived alone, as his marriage with Glenda had produced only one child, and the judge had produced a piece of paper that granted him minimal custody. Because he was—as evidenced by an extensive investigation into his inability to hold down a job or drive across town without taking anxiety pills—*sick in the head.* Of course the official document said it with more tact, though the words, "... due to his infirm mental state ... ," were all he could recall.

He heard the couch springs shift and hastened to pop the toaster, pull out the slightly browned rye, scoop up the bacon with the miniature black spatula whose tip was melted from careless cooking some week back, and assemble her sandwich. *How could I have missed this?* he asked himself, staring in disbelief at the bag of thrice-washed, pre-chopped lettuce. Most of the chunks were brown around the edges. But Dalton went to work, arranging the little slivers of iceberg so that only the choicest edges hung over the bread crust. Thanking God for the massive tomatoes whose size had, when he stood at the checkout in the supermarket, left him strangely unsettled. One of them he couldn't even palm. Now they covered the lettuce generously, and as Marie rounded the corner he was just finishing the masterwork, tucking the crumbled bacon into the tomato slice's little seeded cavities.

"Glenda says I should try him out," Marie said in a voice strained more with exhaustion than boredom as she pulled out her chair with the proper etiquette that was her mother's signature. She sat spine-straight, aligned with but not resting against the chair back.

"Try who?" Dalton asked, his face stretched so that his intersecting wrinkles confronted her with a terrible geometry as he laid his offering on the mustard-colored cloth that barely covered the table. He thought that maybe he had tuned out momentarily, as happened often when he was focused on the simplest task. Years ago his boss had asked him to put in a bare minimum of nine hours per day to compensate for his inevitable drifting. As this was when the lawyer-mediated divorce sessions were in full season, but he and Glenda had not yet physically separated, he took this as a chance to pass on his boss's mandate that he stay from eight to six, rounding that nine up to an even ten.

"The boy she's dug up for me." Since their divorce Glenda had taken it upon herself to secure for her daughter a regular supply of *boys,* who were actually men—always barely under eighteen and always older in appearance than in actuality. Each candidate was a blend of attractive and fatherly in slightly different configurations—sometimes broad shoulders and moderately condescending tones, sometimes wildly encouraging and career-oriented if host to a ruthless rash of pimples. Marie failed to share details of these encounters with her father, but this was largely because, one by one, within five minutes she gave a "Pleased to meet you, but I got a terrible migraine coming on," at which point she would do things even more outrageous than her mother could ever have proposed.

"I thought maybe you meant a doctor. For that—for the staph infection." Marie had contracted MRSA staph in her armpit—who knew how—some months back. Boils that looked like dark Greek olives sprouted between her arm and breast. After six specialists and eleven types of antibiotics, the doctors turned her over to a homeopath who had her spreading marigold and some sort of rare New Zealand honey over the infected area. And it worked. But only for a week. And then the purple lumps returned, first with an annoying pulse and, within hours, with an agonizing pain that stole her attention from anything else and brought her to bed.

"That's the thing. I mean, either way, I'm not sleeping with a single some*body* she tries to set me up with," Marie carried on sneeringly. "Either way, I'm not going to *try him out*, but I can't believe that she's suggesting it. Then she starts going into detail, telling me about positions and I walked out. Get enough of that at school, mom. That's why I was late. To you. Sorry for being quiet when you asked me earlier. I'm just . . . I missed my first bus because I've been staying with a friend for the past few days, and I underestimated the amount of time it would take to get me from her house to the station."

This was the first time Marie had spoken of Glenda, except in passing or due to technical necessity, since the divorce. Dalton found himself slumped over involuntarily, his stomach as tight as a new, unopened flour sack. He leaned against the counter for support, and counted the seconds of his inhales to regulate his rapid heart. How strange that this woman sitting at his table was his own daughter. He listened as her teeth pierced the bread and clamped down on the hardened bacon, feeling some small satisfaction that she was rebelling against Glenda. For while Glenda knew that her daughter smoked and ate red meat at her father's apartment—in spite of Marie's abundant application of perfume or menthol to her chin, collar, and, if she'd chain smoked, to her tongue—she never spoke of these things aloud. She merely clipped out articles about lung cancer and meat consumption from *A New You: Fitter, Happier, More Productive* on the kitchen table and set them on the table. Before breakfast and dinner. The same mother who placed condoms under her *dear one's* pillow.

A FEW hours later, as Marie sat smoking on the apartment porch, with both the screen and the storm doors closed, Dalton called Glenda.

20

"Try him out," he said, his voice monotone, avoiding the ascension that would have signaled a snide question.

"It's better than the fanatical shit you're feeding her, Dal," Glenda said, her fingernails tapping rhythmically on the marble counter Dalton had installed in their home.

"*What?*" The word came out in a shriek, and he saw himself forty years younger in a red-floored kitchen lined with looming yellow cabinets. Feigning idiocy before his mother's allegations. Only this time nothing was feigned.

"You know *very well*. She denied it, but I know it was you. Went and found God after we split up. Very original. But don't you *dare* drag her into your God trip."

"*What?*" he asked again, unable to say more, a sensation like the heartburn he had when he ate a grapefruit too fast, squeezing his stomach and burning his esophagus.

"Mary Margaret Alacoque. Or whatever her name is." And then she made that *tst* sound, the one that used to make him laugh mid-fight. The one that felt like nerve gas, now, eliciting a shiver in the hand that held the phone.

But Dalton bit his tongue and felt all of his restraint bleed out in an instant.

"What the hell you talking about, Glenda? Margaret Mary who? What kind of—"

"Some *saint*," Glenda said. "I caught her reading it. In fact I don't know if she's been doing much of anything else. Don't tell me you don't know what I'm talking about."

"I don't."

"*Don't.*"

"Don't."

"So you haven't gone and done the old born again number?"

"No."

"Well then *who's?*"

"Yes. Who *is* this Margaret All-a-coke?"

"Well, that's why I figured *you'd* set her up with the book.

Some nun who flagellated her own shoulders and back, pricked herself until the blood came out in the name of *Jesus*, talked to paintings of some Francis Sales guy, saw, supposedly, that Sacred Heart I'm sure you've seen it if you saw it you'd know it I looked it up on the internet. Clearly not right in the head. Nope. Which is why I thought that *you*—"

Dalton ducked below her blow, closed his eyes and saw himself walking down a long hall as his boss escorted him out of the office and out of another job.

"How'd you get to be such an expert on her?" he asked.

"I read the book while Maric was asleep the other night. Couldn't put it down I was so disturbed. I even accidentally underlined some parts. So God help me when Marie picks up on my spying. Then, Jesus. Then I don't even know. My parents spied on me and you know well what it did to *me*."

"Well, look, let's just keep this between you and me. I'll be watching."

"Alright then, alright, Dal. *Tst.* You alright, Dal? You sound—"

"I am," he said, and watched his hand hang the phone on the wall, watched the device crush the button that cut his connection to the woman whose bed he'd shared for so many years. The softest downy blankets, scarlet comforters and eggshell sheets. The things she wore and the things he swore underneath.

LATER, after he and Marie played their traditional Saturday night game of Scrabble, Dalton made a pot of coffee, double the grounds. Regular. But he laid the orange decaffeinated bag across the counter so as not to stoke her suspicions. She had certainly stirred his, with her strange contributions to Scrabble. *Sanctity* and *poverty* sharing the same *y*. *Sacre Coeur.*

"What's that?" he had asked, staring at the foreign words.

"French," she said. "For *Sacred Heart.*"

He frowned, ran his index finger over the crease.

"It's a famous tourist place," she assured him, "in Paris."

But he thought he heard her mutter, under her breath, *plgrmj*.

The coffee, then, was a necessity. Stress always made him sleepy, and he didn't care if he had to offset what the caffeine did to him with one of the cigarettes he'd bought for his daughter at the gas station. Jeez. Eight dollars a pack, though. Now if there was such a thing as *sin* it was charging poor ordinary people eight dollars for the only thing that'll get 'em through the night. At midnight he consumed his third cup of coffee. The roast was acidic and he reached his jittery hands into the cabinet, feeling for the old bottle he knew without seeing, the prescription stomach tablets that Glenda had found for him from some homeopathic doctor; they wouldn't interfere with his other medications, she told him. They tasted sweet, even sweeter than the creamer he'd used to try and dull the coffee's bitter bite. And in his mouth he almost felt Glenda's disembodied tongue. His eyes closed. His heart hurt. *Sacre Coeur. Cordelia,* he said, remembering the poor production of *Lear* that signified so little in spite of his high school drama teacher's tireless coaching and sacrifice. He drank and chewed in the dark kitchen, seeing what he could see by nothing more than the meager offerings of the streetlights outside. Seeing, in a half-hallucinatory moment, one of Marie's childhood pictures—of an oblong sun, marmalade and mad, swirling through the sky, as stick figures bent low below—on the refrigerator.

When at last he steadied himself enough to move toward her room, he walked on tiptoes. Living alone, however, and never having spied on his daughter before, he had not memorized the creaky spots, which were many. A minefield of creaks. Fifteen minutes from the kitchen to her bedroom down the hall.

Perhaps it was these small wails under his feet, like the protests of the damned, that had woken her. Or perhaps she was a closet insomniac. For when he turned the handle without any noticeable noise, and shoved the door open, she was sitting there, reading something by the light of the blinking bar sign outside.

As she moved from barely discernible blur to flesh of his flesh he saw that a strange, saw-dust colored cloth covered her body.

"You okay?" she asked, just as he opened his mouth to ask the same.

"What you reading?" he responded, flipping the light switch up and sending both of their fingers over both of their eyes.

"Oh. An old book. Belonged to Glenda's mom." She buried the black, hardcover book under her pillow even as the scent— that oldbook admixture of faint clove and death—perfumed the room.

Glenda's mother—whom he knew next to nothing of, so thick was the quiet that shrouded her—had died in childbirth, bringing Glenda into the world.

"*What're you wearing?*"

Marie had tried to cover her shoulders with the baby blue blanket that he had washed for her, hung to dry, and then dotted with her favorite essential oil—sandalwood—in preparation for her stay. He saw her inhaling the still-pungent scent and smiled a little.

"Oh. This. A potato sack," she said. "Mom, um, Glenda—"

"It's okay." It was not okay. He held onto his head as though it would detach at any moment.

"Glenda gets these big bags of potatoes. Gluten free diet or something."

"Oh." Glenda. Glenda. *So, how'd you get the name Glenda? Oh, that. Something I've got to live with. My father named me after some Hollywood actress. My mom died in childbirth. But let's not talk about that.*

Let's not talk about that. One of her favorite phrases. He meandered, with firm intent and interest but scratching his head as though aloof, to the edge of her bed. And then he saw it. Jutting out from beneath the blanket like a red blade of grass. Poking above the neck-slit she'd cut into the tan sack. The obvious coarseness of the sack made Dalton itch. The scarlet slash across her skin made him sick.

"I'm sorry," she said. "I don't think you'll get it, Dad. This is something I think I have to do alone." She was never like this. Never *needed to do this on my own.*

"Honey," he said, his eyes filling with filmy liquid, "honey, you don't have to do *anything* alone." Dalton reached over the bed awkwardly, his elbow knocking her raised knee as he touched her cheek.

And then, as though to fend off his attempts at succor, Marie pulled the potato sack down around her shoulders, the neck slit she'd cut tearing down the middle. There. He saw it. Just above her left breast, which, almost exposed, drew a sheet of sweat across his lower back, made him shiver and turn momentarily away. There, just below her collar bone, he saw that the red slash led to a red blotch. Shaped like nothing in particular. Then, as he stared, shaped like a heart circled with electrical wires or the twine he used to use to tie the Christmas tree to the top of the station wagon, the frayed kind that always made the whole trip feel quaint. But this, whatever it *was*, was decidedly *not* quaint. Topped with two perpendicular lines something like the realtor's sign holder they'd placed in their lawn when they thought they could find a buyer for *their* house in spite of the awful market, a buyer who would dissolve what they shared physically into the loose and fluid medium of money. Which was easier to hide. Marie looked at him with wide eyes. Hiding nothing.

"I didn't do it," she said.

"What?" His fingers fell from her cheek to the scar. As he touched it a terrible tingle shocked his heart. She went on.

"It was just there. One morning. Maybe the potato sack scratched it."

"Why are you *wearing* that thing?" he asked.

"Dad. I can't," she said. "It wouldn't be possible. To understand. I love you. I never told you, tell you. But I love you. I love you. I do."

The taste of bacon crept up his throat and his hands went

down around his stomach. Never in his life had he been able to cry. At least not since he was eight-years old. And this was no exception.

"GLENDA?" His voice was dried, deep and thirsty, the way coffee always made it.

"You're up early," she said.

"I've been up all night."

He had settled at the edge of the old recliner—the one that used to be in the garage, when they all three lived together—in the living room, surprised at how quickly his daughter's breathing became rhythmic and sleep-filled in the next room. Just minutes after he left. *Surrender*, he thought. *To what? Who? Or—to whom? However you say it. Help!*

"Listen, Dal, you know it's not good for you, or for me, to have you coming to me with your problems."

"No. It's Marie. She's not right. Mentally I mean. Do you know she sleeps—"

"Dal. Don't be puritanical. I'm perfectly *fine* with the idea of her 'sleeping around,' or whatever they're calling it now. It's good for her to get a broad sense of the possibilities. I'm not saying anything new when I note that this was precisely one of our problems: we'd experienced only each other. And I won't have her go down that road. We know where it leads, Dal. Don't we. So, if you're shocked, I'm sorry and all that. But I'm perfectly *fine* with the idea. So long as she takes all the precautions."

Silence. His fingers scrambled the letters laid out on the Scrabble board. They turned *Sacre Coeur* into *Our Crease* as he touched the terrible geometry that furrowed into his forehead again.

"No. She sleeps in a potato sack. Says it—or something, but not her—left these red creases across her chest. I think she's. Maybe cutting herself." But, as he said this, he doubted. And trusted his daughter.

"That's that penance bullshit in that Mary Alacoque book."

"The book belonged to your mother."

Silence. The sun broke into the apartment, its rose-colored fingers touching his face and giving him the succor he'd tried to give Marie. It looked like a ball in a child's drawing as the heat-waves that rose from where it melted the tarmac sent strange fumes back up and made it blurry.

"I think we need to seriously consider in-patient care. I'm serious, Dal, and I'm not budging. I've been waiting for this to happen and now here it is. God. Genetics," she said, and when she said this he felt his stomach cave in entirely, felt his lips against his blue-jeaned knee, saw the phone fall and then crack against the varnished floor. Saw the sun swirl madly toward him.

MARIE found him there when she woke some hours later. No pulse. His arm outstretched. Just beyond the limp, cupped, desperate-as-starving-animal fingers she saw little pieces of scrabble at the tips of his fingers, just beyond reach: Sacre Co. She opened his limp-but-clasped fingers. Found the letters *r-u-e* tucked there. He still had work to do. Her eyes hankered after the phone. To call. Who? She could not find the phone. She could not even think.

And the wreathe of thorns that had been there who knew how long but which she had only of late come to feel, pricking with each breath, around her own heart, the wreathe of thorns pressed and pricked tighter than ever. Then, as with some difficulty she managed to free a long-held breath, one by one the thorns burst from her and scattered to the ground, blending there with Dalton's letters. Several thorns bounced from the floor and fell into her hands. Marie held the sharp things, scrutinizing each piece like a skeptical medieval monk who, accustomed to doubting the very relics he dealt in, is finally persuaded by the faith of those who come to see them.

Copper

BRIAN CAME IN for a hygiene kit and a cot, *just even for a night*. All we had were the small ladies' deodorant, child-sized toothbrushes, and flavorless floss. Brian had come late, in fact his knuckles knocked the door just as I was going to shut it. I checked his last name and began to finger through our files, careful not to give the impression that I wasn't listening.

He used to rip copper from cold houses in the gutted city, take it to the south end where you could turn it into cash. Drag the screeching braids of wires along the gutters and back alleys, dodging cops and children. Now he drives trucks from the cold plains of North Dakota to the cool coffee shop districts of Seattle, takes sunflowers to bakeries where they meld it into cookies they sell for five dollars each, the copper-colored circles, five hundred pennies for one.

He told me, fingering a crucifix and a self-rolled cigarette, that his family is talking to him again now that his wandering comes with a paycheck every two weeks. He sends half of it home to atone. Goes to the bank and turns cash into pennies, rolls and rolls of them, trying to figure how, he told me, how he would have paid his folks if he were still a child: rolls and rolls of them, remembering how many times when he was small his father said to his mother *I don't know why we had him in the first place,* under the living room lamp that buzzed, its copper-colored exterior such that you could see your face there, could see yourself doing a lot of dying there, in the living room.

But now it was time to do some living. *Put off the old man. Put on the new one.* What he said.

You don't know what the road can do to you, he said, *I just need a break. For a day. Called in sick again. But I'll be back behind the wheel tomorrow.*

I checked his records. He was here for three years five years ago. "Just one night," I said, feeling like a dealer pushing dope.

Brian pulled out a fork, knife, and spoon, coppery heirlooms. *Brought my own utensils* he said, a dulled but still kicking pride pulsing just behind his eyes. I knew that all he wanted was food, but the way he gripped that knife I had to force myself to keep breathing, stop holding my breath. He looked at me until my gaze stopped poking around, until I really saw him. Then he stood up, staring at an abandoned building across the street, peering in through the absolute dark, through those windows and through those walls, and I saw him sit back for the first time, relaxed except for his grip around the knife. But I knew now he would not hurt me. I moved my fingers away from the alarm button toward which they had crawled without my even knowing it.

He stood up, pocketed the knife, and reached out his hand for a shake that nearly broke my own. And then he was gone.

LATER, walking to the bus, I passed that old building, fingering the loose pennies in my pocket, useless things that counted for nothing. On tiptoes I looked in upon the abandoned, absolute dark. Scratching sounds came from within, scraping and scratching and swearing. And a laugh that I have gone looking for since. A laugh that only children seem capable of, unmixed with repression or violence, followed by a *Put off the old man.*

I tossed the pennies through the window, and listened to them land in anti-climactic clinks upon a hardwood floor within. It didn't do what I was hoping it would. To my heart.

Control

The setting of thine eye and cheek proclaim
A matter from thee, and a birth, indeed
Which throes thee much to yield.
—Sebastian, from Shakespeare's *The Tempest*

FIVE MINUTES AFTER the first time I killed a man, I found out
how easy the whole ordeal could be. Killing, dying, and all that.
The way the cessation of this large man's life stilled my wild
grasping to control my own beating heart (in spite of the fact that
I never felt so fearful as when in the silence I could sense my
blood pulsing) and my own craze for consciousness (in spite of
the fact that too much consciousness was what kept me self-med-
icating). As he lay there, bloated on the asphalt in broad daylight,
the crosswalk framing his wide body like police chalk, I dragged
my numb leg across the pavement and cradled him in my arms,
mourning like the plaster Pietà my mother kept in the long back
hallway and humming old hymns I'd learned in grade school and
hadn't sung since. An octopus of arms grabbed at me, disembodied voices saying, "Stop."

Later that day, in a shared hospital room halved by no more
than a dense drape, Cecilia Jade consoled me. She said—without
whispering or muffling her voice—that medical professionals can
come to no consensus on the definition of *life*, that her friend is a
doctor (so she knows), that the definition of *death* is contingent
upon the definition of life, that though my guilt felt real it was

really a matter of semantics. This only made me feel sick for the cancer patient on the other side of the drape. Not wanting Cecilia to storm out and away forever onto some eternal circuit of elevated trains and inter-city buses, our three-month child still (so far as I knew) stewing in her womb, I only nodded. After visiting hours ended her terrible vigil, I sucked down the ice cream centers of three foam discs in fright, discarded the extra firm mashed potatoes placed delicately before me, saw that Cecilia left her purse by accident or as a promise, and, around midnight, the nurse placed pills on my tongue that stopped my shaking and put me to sleep.

CECILIA Jade was working the night shift at the twenty-four-hour diner stuck onto the end of a long strip mall. She was making $2.33 per hour plus tips. *The Grind* it was called, though it wasn't a strip club, in spite of all connotations to the contrary. Some ordinance kept gentlemen's clubs outside the city limits. And then, as though a huge stray cat had crept out there to give birth, a whole litter of them popped up, a whole lit-up neon dysfunctional family of them, with names like *The Lion's Den* and *Sugar and Spice*, little places all of them that seemed harmless in their smallness and their separateness. But if a man drove by them late at night, a steady beaming stream of them————.

When I first met Cecilia she told me, her mouth drizzling too-hot tomato soup out over her still-redder lipstick, that she had done her time in *that* line of work but was finished with it. Was done with how many husbands waiting for her in the parking lot come closing time, husbands who sometimes fondled roses raised by the retired teacher who kept the a quaint greenhouse at the other edge of town, others waiting without the play, their sweaty fists filled with folded cash. Still, even when we lived together and she was doing time at *The Grind,* she swore she made more—up to $20 an hour—the less she wore, and she repeated this on those nights her spoils only rounded out to minimum wage. When she said this she would look at me as though I had no face. When she said this I would fixate on our wall where the plaster bled out like the ooze that covers a wound. Every day she caught the last running bus to "open" the late shift and the first running bus to come home. I worked from home in those days for a headhunting company, making calls on behalf of hospitals looking to hire freshly minted doctors. Four years spent studying history and here I was, fading into its unwritten annals. I spent my days, like her, telling people what they wanted to hear. Perhaps that's why I'm deaf now. Or it could be the firecracker. But I'll get to that in a moment.

Cecilia Jade and I lived in a studio across the street from a man now known as a serial killer. A kindly man who always nodded when you walked past and never seemed as cynical as he should have been considering the world's wracked state. He looked out upon everything and everyone owning the same scientific wonder with which in childhood I had looked upon the ants in the red plastic kit given me by my father. He was a little shorter than the good Lord intended but with the good appetite the same good Lord gave him. That's how my grandmother taught me to speak of fat people. She also told me that fat people tend to be nice because they have nothing else going for them. She also wrapped her waist in a belt after each child she birthed and held her breath until her shape came back.

Anyhow, our old neighbor serial killer—Kellogg Mink was his name—was a smart man, too. You could tell when you watched him standing there holding his hose. You could tell he knew what this world's about from the piles and piles of newspapers and magazines stacked by mailmen on his porch. You could see in his darkened eyes that his head was filled with brilliant things too grand for me. You could even tell he knew too much, because he couldn't hold a conversation.

I wish now I would have asked him something, figured out what magazines he subscribed to exactly, read them and worked some article he'd know—or even ones he'd written—into a passing conversation. For he wrote many, many articles in popular psychology magazines, one of which everyone knows now. It's titled "Napoleon's Childhood." Cecilia convinced me his death was also our mistake. She said it's best to make people feel needed, even if for all you care they could curl up and die.

"Take the most pathetic person you know," she said, sitting on the edge of the exposed mattress, sheet-edge scrunched in her fist, mindlessly scanning the op-ed pages of a magazine. "Make him feel like he's your prosthetic leg, like without him you'd be a cripple. You'll feel good about it, too," she said, standing, then sitting back in the leather chair until her skinny little body was buried in that big thing. It squished and squeaked like a trapped mouse, that big chair set out on the serial killer's lawn after they had emptied his house, after he was put in jail for something like 137 years like he'd outlive Noah for God's sake.

Kellogg Mink. Once, long before reporters called him horrifyingly clever things like *The Nearly Extinct American Mink*, one Halloween a group of neighborhood teenagers dressed up like minks and converged on him and tackled him as he stood there tending to the thirst of his little blades of grass. I've never heard anyone cry the way he did when they toppled him. He cried as though for the first time, out of sheer happiness rather than nervousness and to mask angst. I've been listening for that cry ever since.

EXCEPT for Mink, people didn't do things like that in our neighborhood. Tend their grass. Come outside. At night you could count some seventy TVs in the eight story high rise across the way alone, but I'd bet my bottom dollar those same screens were humming all day long, like the stars just beyond our vision—hidden only by a bigger light. In the Midwest, at least in *that* Midwest, in Mill City proper, no one snubbed their noses at a malnourished lawn, even if it were hay-yellow and ready for the Living Nativity they acted out on the end of the strip mall opposite *The Grind*. Of course a nativity scene would have looked entirely out of place on Mink's lawn. No holy family there. He believed in science, and was a serial killer besides. And in those days people were hung up on this silly line of demarcation, certain as the Tropic of Cancer: north of it lived all the folks who believed in God, and south all those who believed in science.

Speaking of nativities, about that time Cecilia was pregnant. She had gone in to the clinic for one counseling session and the woman with the pin reading <u>MY</u> HEALTH said the surgery would be subsidized. That's what they called it. *Subsidized surgery.* I can't count how many times I heard it called that. I was supposed to sit in the waiting room but as the video on hysterectomies they showed was plotless and the magazine maidens were hopelessly airbrushed and I was the only one there, and as Cecilia had scheduled an appointment for 7:30 a.m., with no security guards in sight, I put my ear against door 103 and heard *subsidized surgery* and *privacy* and *once-a-year-shot* and *just what I needed* and to this day can't say why I found myself kneeling down there at the base of the door, the pale gold floor blurring before me, looking now like strands of floating hay and me playing the part and only playing the part of some unwitting angel of God muttering "Be not afraid!" as the door opened and Cecilia's eyes closed at the sight of me. "Are you comfortable?" the counselor asked, her fingers curled around Cecilia's forearm and her eyes pinching until her squint pierced me and she said very professionally, "We also offer counseling services for men at our Third Street Clinic."

And though she didn't touch me, she squeezed the answer out of me: "I'll never sleep with someone again," to which she let out a little puffed-up cloud of a laugh. But my answer remains true to this day.

Cecilia was so mad she sat in the backseat of the car and said nothing the whole drive home. Meanwhile I died with each noisy breath she took because though the nurse who checked her vitals in the hall said "very good" to both pulse and blood pressure, I

was sure she would simply disintegrate. Get edited out. Like a
line in an S.O.S., sent to God or whomever, that gets cut because
it says too much—words so fleshy they might as well be a human
being. I felt overwhelmed by what she spelled and doubly so by
my power to remove her from my life. Find work a few states
away and forge some great new statue called Forgetfulness.

In short, I felt huge in my capacity to make her disappear
completely. When at last I looked into the rear view mirror I saw
Cecilia sleeping, drooling like a baby there, and like a good parent
I drove around and around the same block, counting the number
of Republican and Democrat posters on the lawns, the number of
fingers on my hands, the number of years since I'd lost my virgin-
ity, stopped believing in or at least stopped worrying over God,
called my mother in her Ohio retirement home, until Cecilia
woke and asked if I could make her French toast. I remembered
something my father said once when my mother, on a lazy Saturday, asked him the same question. I said I was an American and
was insulted, and we laughed and lost the weight for a few minutes until she said, "What was that 'Be not afraid' bullshit about?"

ON the day of the surgery, some morning later, I woke feeling
my whole life was somehow subsidized by something or someone beyond myself, against my will. But I did not know whom. I
wanted to figure it out, to tell my patron to keep his funds and let
me suffice, alone.

WE held hands the way we had the night we met and went for a
walk that lasted three hours. This time our walk was much
shorter, stretching some fifty feet to the car—a dull red Corolla
whose back window was covered with indecipherable, sun-
washed bumper stickers we had wasted a whole weekend failing
to remove—to our very different destiny. One of oldest ones read
Keep America Pure With———, the last word blanched deceased.
Still, as her palm sweat chilled against mine, I dreamed for one

dumb second that we were heading to my apartment to fall help-lessly in love again.

I tell you, if I understand him correctly (I'm sure Kellogg Mink would have known), that Einstein was on to something at once highfalutin and everyday. Even though our distance was no longer than the 50-foot dash I ran in high school, it took at least half an hour in my head. Cecilia's eyelids were colored purple, her long, thin, lavender scarf veiling her neck and covering her mouth and nose entirely. Only her eyes, like two ellipses, hinted that there was something depressingly desperate beneath the royal purple and the knock-out nonchalance. When, weeks later, I told a mutual friend of this private desperation, she shook her head hotly and said, "Desperation, pff," and said many other things without volume so that only spit came out and salted the sulfur-smelling eggs on both her plate and mine. And she snatched her purse, practiced mindful deep breathing, and gave me a polite "Do take care of yourself," before she departed.

"The child may not even by mine," I told myself, and then my body went numb. From my left toes to my left rib I felt nothing. I fell.

Four competing horns, like the first practice of a teenage jazz quartet. A dying Cadillac shoving its snout under a green pickup. And, like a bunch of day laborers or movie extras, the crowd.

I had seen them there waiting for us. They held plastic con-tainers of water, water my mother, a Catholic, called holy. Their signs played on the Christmas season with nativity scenes, Mary's belly undergoing an ultrasound, a haloed Christ saying *Choose Life*. They converged on me the way I had imagined the children had Mink, at least a dozen dangling rosaries and sprinkling water, muttering *Hail Marys* and Holy Scripture. Their faces stretched to my exhaling consciousness like round raindrops elongating, sur-rounding. But, unlike Mink, I could not laugh, and it killed me. Cecilia was gone. She had crossed to the other side. There, in the center of the street, the other side carried their crosses over to me, dangled their crosses over me. Christ on plastic and silver and golden crosses swinging like pendulums from their fisted rosaries, Christ hanging at the center of the cosmos.

The scream. And I swear I could hear over the screeching rubber the stubs of her half-way-high-heels as they neared the shore of this no man's island. Her clammy hands on my neck. The painted nails of her index fingers piercing into my glands. Choking me. Pulling me from the disaster. Something shoved the whole pile of us forward, moved as though by some tectonic fit. But a single man, a doctor, a very smart and very quiet protester (I later learned), a little shorter than the good Lord intended with a good appetite, went flying, his flabby, failing body carrying the severe energy that some scientists—maybe even Kellogg Mink— call life.

CECILIA Jade went through with it some weeks later. The more I said about providence and promises and paced in our five-by-five kitchen instead of sleeping with her at night, the more she steeled herself and said *bullshit*.

AT NIGHT, when she stopped coming home and sent a letter from Florida saying she'd moved in with the retired father she'd sworn abused her, I started walking to the Holy Cross cemetery, spade in hand, tiptoeing the whole way off the sidewalk where the streetlights couldn't touch me. I cried for her the way Christ cried for Jerusalem. That's what my mother used to tell me when I'd run away at fifteen. *I cried for you the way Christ cried for Jerusalem.* "Christ," I would say, and storm upstairs to my subsidized bedroom. Kneeling next to my father's grave, not in prayer. I promise. I didn't know how to pray. Shoving the steel into the dirt until it started cracking apart. Stabbing it down, the metal apparatus. Stabbing. After some time, in the cruelty of April, I managed to gut a space the size of my canceled child. The night I finished, I pulled out a candle from our junk drawer. *Mine* now I guess. That word. *Mine.* The rent and the food and the empty, elongated capsule of a convex space on my bed. Mine.

I called in sick and fell asleep with the candle in the breast pocket of my shirt. A few days after I had dug the grave clean I woke up nauseous. Hungry, but unable to eat. I snatched a book of matches that read *The Grind* and walked down to the graveyard to hold vigil in the naked brightness of day. No one would notice the light this way. This little light of mine. My hands made a cave around the candle, which was half underground like a living stem. I lit it, got ready to stare at it for an hour the way my mother stared at her wedding candle when my father left this earth. The explosion that bit my ear and screamed until nothing but sirens filled my hearing told me I had grabbed one of the firecrackers Cecilia Jade bought on the Fourth of July and left behind. Slowly, I could make out nothing but the sound of silence, a terrible declaration of independence from the white noise of this world. A sound that has gone from sour to sweet like an apple bitten early but left on the tree until it bruises but ripens entirely. A noise that sometimes speaks in the language of God.

In a Better Place

It would certainly be remarkable, Wittgenstein wrote, *if we had to believe the reliable person who says "I can't be wrong" or who says, "I am not wrong."*

THE MAN'S BLUE SWEATSHIRT is too small. His face does not fit inside the frame of the hood. "He was innocent," he says. "I know he's in a better place." He shakes his head, the top part of his double-chin curving down into a frown. "I just can't believe something like this would happen. Actually, man, I been having a hard time all day being real *sure* that it did happen. I seen that baby smiling all the time. In summer sometime she takes that baby for walks in a stroller. She'd walk so fast almost like she's running. Training for a marathon or somethin'. Chasing. Chased. Somethin' not right." Until now he has averted his gaze, staring anywhere but the eyes of the cameras or reporters, but now he turns to the man with the microphone, the man who nods at his every word, and says, "I mean how, why, how does it happen that someone lets their baby in a room for thirty-eight hours without even checking in one time?"

The reporter shifts as the man, holding the string of his hooded sweatshirt like a child holding the string of a balloon that is about to blow away, says something that the microphone barely catches—"But what does it mean?"—but catches nonetheless.

"Back to you, Megan."

The screen flashes to a lawyer whom reporters have surrounded on his daily run around a lagoon. He smooths down the

41

hood of his black sweatshirt as he talks, says that the autopsy confirms hypothermia as the cause of death. "It seems that the child was left in a room with a space heater on high while the parents made, used, and sold methamphetamine," he says, now running his fingers down the string of his sweatshirt, pulling at it so that the neck tightens, unwittingly swinging the string back and forth in a pendulum motion, as though his head—which seems tanned from some combination of artificial booth light and stints to a Florida beach house—is a muted bell, unable to carry the sound the situation demands.

ELLA edges away from him, and a cool waft immediately fills the space between them. Garrett edges away as well, as though in agreement that their affectionate cuddling in the face of this news story is somehow indecent. The television screen bestows upon each its luminous blue light. When Garrett looks at her, he sees that her high-boned cheeks are red, but that the blue light of the screen makes them look purple, the color of a bruise. She is wearing a winter hat inside. Their paychecks are both due to be deposited in three days. Their last heating bill was four hundred dollars, though they kept the temperature at sixty-two degrees during the day, fifty-seven at night.

"I guess it's *these* ones that really get me. Not the over-the-top disgusting ones where an abuser hides his abductees in an attic for ten years and, once some neighbor discovers them, the girls tell all the world that he used to laugh while he whipped them. I. Don't know why. But it's, those like that Kellogg Mink don't seem so awful." She turns toward the window on the wall, the one over which they draped the scarlet tapestry her grandmother brought back from Russia. It too looks purple in the television light. "*That*," she says, "is disturbing beyond . . . but *these*, where the innocent one dies of a kind of negligence. Where the criminal does what he does only by not doing anything, *these* are the ones that really get me. Wrong by—accident."

"Accident?" he asks, muting the television.

Flash of light. Fade. Photograph of the dead child's parents. Her poorly-parted hair, one eye open only slightly, the other sickeningly wide. Pallid skin and pale lips. Cheeks sunk under high cheekbones, so that, cut from the context, they could be ornamenting the face of a woman walking down a long runway. She, though, has long been running away. And the look in her eye. Anyone can see that she is far enough away from both origin and destination that she has forgotten both what she was running from and where she is going. Behind her posters of video games—little figures with perfect pixilation, rounded faces with red-cheeks that signal happiness—cover the walls, and a substance that looks like the gutted insides of an old mattress is scattered around the room, the once-beautiful feathers seem now alien things, pure fragments of something once whole that, now scattered beyond repair, have ceased to even suggest their once-wholeness. Her right palm holds a distended belly that swells not with the emptiness of a starving child but with that shape which can only mean a child has started to toss and turn inside her.

YESTERDAY Garrett tried to tell three friends that he has lost the capacity to love. Capacity? Will? Desire? The first one, Sam, wandered over to the side bar, asked for a tequila shot, and took a long time sliding it down the counter, pressing his fingers down upon the salt that coated the rim, pausing to savor the sting of each crystal and looking up at the football game in overtime, shouting "It's overtime, just a sec," back to the group of friends, his blue face making him look cold as they peered upon him from the near-darkness of their corner table. Garrett's head, positioned just beneath the dart board bullseye, saw something in Sam's eyes that made him duck. Jerome, who had only recently asked—a tinge of fear at his forthcoming fortieth birthday?—that they start calling him by his high school nickname of J.D., looked down at his shoes and said, "You have to have courage." Garrett does not disagree. But the manner of J.D.'s saying it, how utterly clear it was that J.D., who was a youth counsellor, had said the same thing to seven hundred young men who have come to him by force or desperation. A definitive tone that betrays a calm refusal to *see*, to *know* the terrible revelation that sits just across the table, that looks down at one's own shoes but refuses to look down into the abyss over which the person sits, balanced precariously atop a barstool.

YESTERDAY, Garrett asked her if she would ever change her mind about bringing a child into the world. He watches her now, watches her eyes fixate on the woman's swelled belly, and inches toward her until the channel of cold that had cut between them is no more. The cold is all around them but not between them.

The screen is dazzling white, but only for a second, and then BREAKING NEWS appears in a font at once bubbling and commanding. She mutes the volume and takes his hand and lifts it, he thinks, toward her belly, but she continues to lift it until it reaches her left temple, and presses it there.

On the screen a *private* phone recording of a darkened apartment complex in Paris jitters, as though the hand that holds it is also chilled, unsteadied by cold. Then a surge, an explosion of brilliant white, like that decadent firework his father would save for last, would pull out of his pocket after pretending they had lit them all off, and then, before they could adjust to the fact that all was not finished, he would let it explode, filling up the backyard. The volume is muted. As a child, this is what his parents did. A kind of compromise struck between reverence for time with family and the very real incapacity of each to *be* with their own children for more than a few minutes without some sort of distraction. Every conversation they had about their days for all those years layered with ten thousand images flashed across the screen.

The news station plays the video again, this time in slow motion, and with his free hand he reaches over for hers, finds the remote there and turns on the volume.

A terrorist blew herself up in Paris. That brilliant comet was her body.

"Awful," she says.

"I'm—. I'm not sure I know what it means."

"Someone died."

"Yeah, but the whole thing—I would need to know so much more for it to mean more than an... I can't quite say senseless, because by tomorrow we'll probably have ten reasons for her motives, a pieced-together biography. But that doesn't... We just watch... this. Act. Like it's senseless, random chaos. She had a life. Somehow got to this point. Was brought to or brought herself to in ten thousand intersecting ways."

"What if it's not so complicated?"

"Chaos is complicated."

"What if that's all it is? A little chaos?"

"Someone died."

"What do you want to do, come to understand her beliefs so that you can feel some sort of—sympathy?"

"The direful spectacle of the wrack, which touched the very virtue of compassion in thee..."

"What?"

"Nothing. You're right. Sympathy—that's not the thing. As isn't understanding the terrorist's beliefs. Knowing them all. Having a grasp of each piece. All except for the *actual belief.* Which I couldn't have if I wanted it."

"But you would want it?"

"What?"

"Belief."

"Certainty," he said, the edges of his eyes circled, now, with a hot ring of red.

He fell into silence and could not get up from it, out of it, like the child stuck inside the Christmas ball, who stares out from inside knowing nothing he said or even screamed could possibly make sense to those outside.

She dropped his hand delicately, first letting it run down her clavicle, then just above her breast, and then ran her own fingers through her hair. Failing to straighten a snarl, she disappeared from the room, which is to say, the room disappeared from her own vision, and she thrust her hand into a hallway drawer, over-turning the mess of postcards and tea bags and rosewood soap bars her mother sent for her birthdays, until she grasped a blue brush, the same one that she had, in the mirror-absorbed days of adolescence, combed slowly through the then-dyed strawberry blonde strands.

When he saw her holding that brush he shifted in the loveseat, remembering the early years of their marriage, when he would move it through her hair at night and say *I love you* with such certainty.

NOW her own hands moved the beaded teeth of the brush through snarls that snapped with resistance.

"Why are you always so quick to feel sympathy for the rest of the world—literally anyone, but then there's nothing for me, for—how could I bring a child into the world knowing there'd be nothing for her, either?"

Here she fell into silence but for the sound that came when she bit a piece of dangling fingernail. After a time she turned to him, her breath almost visible in the chilled room, and said, "And what does it *do,* anyway, your sympathy for all the world—all the world you never see, touch, or hear?"

HE remembers too much, has many times envied those he visits in nursing homes whose minds are washed with an amnesia always and only understood as a terrible forgetting. But for Gar-rett, ridden with remembering, there was no sense of certainty surrounding that state. Maybe it would be good, even, he now wondered, to drink at least a cupful of the river Lethe. He did not always think this way.

IT is their second dinner together. He is talking quietly but with preoccupied intensity about knowing and not knowing.

"So you were certain of *one* date and you got it wrong, what's the big deal? You're going to lose your mind over getting one date wrong, call into question your entire faculty of judgment? Would you say that about other people? Me? If I get one thing wrong will you distrust all I say?"

"…"

"I…"

"I just—if the best we can do is say, 'I am of the strong opinion that…' or 'I have the unshakable belief that…' If that's all we can do, if that's all we can say, as close as we can come to *certainty,* then;"

She takes the palm of his hand and presses it to her ear.

"Don't tell me you love me," she said. "I can't hear you. And I wouldn't believe you anyway."

He tries to shut out the pulses of blood that he feels as they flush her ears red, tries to shut out what he knows when he touches her.

"But I love you."

"What do you *mean* you love me?" she asks, not to tease or torment him but because she already knows that unless they tease out the *meaning* then later he will call his own claim into question.

"BUT is it really sympathy?" he asks, now, standing up and turning from her, spine bones poking through his shirt as he stretches and turns up the heat, and then turning back again. "That's not what I'm after. I mean I agree with you entirely that so much of that is posturing, for the benefit of the sympathizer," he says, with a certain bitterness of tone accompanied by sweat at the base of his neck, a bitterness that she can't help but find pitiable. "Still, it might be good to sympathize even if we don't do anything," he goes on. "Or maybe sympathy just *is*. Not really a thought-through choice but a feeling more. But how can you not feel something for her?"

"And what if on some level she's the one who did it, in the end, actually?"

"…"

"I mean what if your feeling so sorry is put toward the wrong person? I mean what if it just *isn't* how you say it is and you're—"

"You got it," he said after a span where they sat listening to the radiator rattle like a round of semiautomatic gunshots fired off in the distance, in someone else's world. "There's something there. Something that has something to do with—my. Sometimes. Not. Wanting. To. Live."

His shoulders tense into a defensive barracks, then collapse as he falls to the couch like a dead thing draped across her lap. She drops her knuckle until it touches his lips just barely.

"You turned up the heat," she says.

"Forget about the always-saving-for-some-future-need phase. When are we gonna stop hedging our bets," he whispers, the words barely making it out of his mouth.

"Oh," she says.

"You don't really want me to sympathize with you," he says, as the screen shows a child pulled from a collapsed building in Aleppo, a two-year-old whose face is covered with a thick coat of crumbled concrete except for her mouth, which is red and open but silent, as though the little one is unsure whether she is alive or dead, unsure whether this is really happening.

"I could be better about doing those things people say comprise that thing called love."

"Forget about people," she says, at that precise second making eye contact with the little girl in Aleppo, who looks out as though directly at her.

"Let's go to bed," she says, and, after they both lay there in silence for a long hour, she almost prays. *Good God can you hear a damn thing, God. Are you there with that girl or no and if so how so?*

And if not how can I know, how can I know *you will be here?* and then she reaches across the icy outside of the blanket but cannot find his body, cannot find him under the blanket they had bought at the start of winter, the one whose feathers have allowed them to keep the temperature low, and pulls him closer as a vision of the woman with the sallow face, the methamphetamine glaze over her eyes flashes as though across the ceiling, and she feels as though their bed itself will explode, and all of the feathers will scatter in soft chaos across the room. The woman with the methamphetamine eyes fades, moving backward into what appears to be a jail cell. Once inside, she smiles.

How can I know you will be here? she asks again.

Another hour passes and he has rolled, in his sleep, almost against her. Light sleeper that he is, she can wake him with a little kiss on the nape of his neck. Half-awake he begins to roll over, then reaches for something. But she catches his hand, the line between her lips straining as she studies the strange latex film that had until now separated them, then tosses it into the little purple garbage can next to her side of the bed.

And she knows him for certain. And he knows her for the first time, and yet it is not like the thrill that comes from moving to a new city and being known by no one, free from all recognition, the strange pleasure of being both here and not. It is not like that. Not at all.

Throw Away the Ladder

He must, so to speak, throw away the ladder after he has climbed up it.

—Ludwig Wittgenstein

WHEN AT LAST I saw him, Michelle and I were sitting in a restaurant called *Ask,* a fine, dim place meant for couples who want solitude in public, who want to speak without being heard—the sort of place whose patrons are comprised of one-part extramarital affairs and one-part shy types who need a space in which mumbles aren't drowned in the music. With great delicacy the owner had spaced the tables some five feet apart in spite of the cuts this meant for business, although the cost of cutlets and salads registered this luxury within the form of inflation.

I had not seen my father in fifteen years, and somehow it was fitting that our reunion began with a glimpse of him in Michelle's outstretched spoon, hovering just above the rich white sauce that promised to dress the naked poultry in a mantle of delight. A noisy inhale followed my spotting his long face refracted within the oval frame—do you know how this is, the way you can recognize those close to you even by a shadow, even in a disfigured reflection?—after which I feigned choking, which was less embarrassing than the actual dilemma at hand. Horseradish stung my nose with such severity that real tears appeared under my eyes.

Dad left as he did to find some glowing orb of promise that had been a stone's throw away before a string of us children came and first stalled, then tripped him in his tracks. At some point he picked himself up, looked down at the dust that painted his knees from the fall, glanced at the five faces that contorted back at him a prescient anger over the already-appraised abandonment, grinned in nervous denial of the claims we placed upon him, and picked up the search.

My first thought was that dad's working here, after all these years still threading his rent checks by on-again/off-again stints in the service industry, in no way proved that he had lost the search after all. You could find what he was after in any old hole-in-the-wall, any drug store or semi-hip spot that, like *Ask*, is even ideal for someone on the search, filled as it is with so many souls openly grappling with *the* questions, those eternal questions we do a pretty good job of masking with the old perfume of routine and niceties, even if occasions for their spilling out here were stomach-dropping.

For the next several minutes I was horribly distracted, or, rather, superbly focused on one thing, something years of hitting social media pretty hard—using it during work and when done, done with work and done with dating for a time and so self-banished to a studio apartment so quiet you could hear the heat pulse through the radiators like blood to a broken heart—had sapped. Picking at my sock to enable a broader look around. Handing Michelle my phone and asking her to admire a picture of my niece hanging from a tree branch beside that brother of mine who most perfectly carried our father's mold, this distraction giving me a chance to crane a gaze at the faces of cooks of whom I'd previously only seen as white-capped blurs laboring in the unreality of the hidden kitchen. Hailing the waitress in order to speak directly to her about the meal, asking for ingredients and sending compliments to chefs, all in order to look steadily over her shoulder, until at last I saw him straight through the circular kitchen window.

First his wry, winning smile, the way his teeth showed only through the left side of his mouth, the right half sewn shut in a manner that made happiness seem a transgression he alone had mastered with such aplomb. His mouth always the most prominent, as though the orifice itself had this oracular quality—anything uttered from it charged with a divine truth. And then the shock of black hair still cut close and combed along the sides, curly and unkempt on the top, the twisted mop crying out in dad's autograph of agonized exhilaration. A dishwasher's apron the color of baby's breath covered his still-lanky body, was painted with blotches reminiscent of those that covered his clothes after our early morning hikes through alleyways where we foraged through things set out as trash, my next-youngest brother Sammy and I lurching along to the tune of his raspy promises. The sound of undiluted eagerness assured all the world that here was an accidentally-discarded child of the gods, a bastard child, maybe, but still filled with holy blood. His inheritance was absolutely *real*, was only misplaced, lost, and it was only a matter of taking the right turn, turning over the right trash can lid, or overhearing the right hint buried in a domestic spat seeping with the kettle's steam out the cracked window of a neighbor, and—bliss.

By extension, some share of this bliss should have been our promise as well. But belief in its eventual materialization never took hold of me. Some of my other siblings went chasing either for the gleam that our father had in his eye, or the elusive horde that his eye supposedly saw, but I remained agnostic for most of my life, turning cold against all such claims, to the point that in the last year I had become a complete doubter.

Until Michelle showed up. Michelle, who, I knew, had seen the gleam too, or had looked for long hours into the eyes of someone who had seen it. This doubt pricked me and drew vials of poisonous anger from my being. And so I'd been able to ask Michelle out for dinner, even though, old fashioned as she is, dates for her lead to marriage, and marriage children, and I knew I would be tempted to depart from her after the manner of my soon-wearied father, even sooner than him, and me unable to even leave an afterglow. At least he had the gleam to keep him going, even when the squall of daily duties by which children are raised chilled him like a week's worth of winter rain in Oregon.

When in silent reverence I would sit with hands folded and remember him zipping up and down any elevated landscape that ran along our daily routes—sometimes actual paper routes, as, Dad said, if we had to keep searching anyhow, we might as well help pay for heat and bread while looking—I never noticed the muted rage that attended these visions, a rage somehow made impossible to detect by my fist-bared resistance against the temptation to lay no blame upon anyone. Even if I had wanted to prod him with my own electric volts of blame, he had been in the world but not of mine. At least, that was how I thought, in those days, those small, small-minded days. *My* world. As though there are how many billions of them, worlds, orbiting through the dark matter, stars, and interstellar spaces bound only by gravity. As though, were it not for gravity, these billions of worlds would flee for blank nooks of the milky ether in which they can achieve full autonomy.

I EXCUSED myself, left Michelle—her brilliant eyes too much to look at for too long—at our high booth along the window, and walked like a ten-year-old during a growth spurt, brain synapses out of touch with the size of my feet, over to the door. I didn't have the ring but was planning on talking about it. She wanted marriage and had been dropping words like *stability* and *commitment* for weeks, even going so far as teaching me the Latin *stabilitas.* Had Michelle been a visiting friend intruding this word into our childhood home, she would have received the reprimand of my father's frown, a furrowed brow that rivals the one Charon reserves for those crossing Styx to the shores of hell. But coming from her mouth now *stabilitas* touched my ears like the hands of a bishop anointing a monk who has pledged his life to the same monastery until his last dust-flecked breath. But I'll return to Michelle—I'll return to Michelle.

EVERYBODY knows that things happen when restaurant staff cross over the border that separates the kitchen from the floor. Behind that door there's slammed pans and laughter, the thrill of swearing at the cook over delayed orders, competitions over who can mock the customers at table A4 best. Slabs of beef get dropped into the grease traps before they're fished out and hung to dry. Frozen chicken patties skid like hockey pucks across the floor, before the cook snatches them up and boils the germs right out of them. Although I cannot universalize the following, it is well known that at the right spots—and *Ask* is one of them— cooks do lines of cocaine between heads of lettuce and bottles of balsamic vinegar. But once they emerge onto the dining room floor, waiters and waitresses elevate food with sudden, straight-backed dignity, a deferential disposition absorbed, it seems, from the light-up plastic wise men statues that interrupt the dark during Christmastide. I saw this all happening, Dad alone unchanging, servers transforming before my very eyes, approaching tables with all the deference we pay them to deliver, stopping just short of kissing rings before they go back there, back to the sarcasm sprinkled over chopped lettuce heads, the salt shaken on the Brussel sprouts that sizzle alongside the coke. But Dad haunted these places because between all of the sweating and the grease, the burnt dinner rolls and the freshly-whipped potatoes, between the work-release dishwasher and the father-of-four sous chef, you would find IT. It was just a matter of staying awake.

MY FATHER himself had stayed away from all hard drugs, and made a big stink of this abstinence during our childhood, waving it around like a soldier's decorative emblem. My father's father was a police officer killed on the job, stabbed by a cocaine addict on a high, hit, one bartender who witnessed the event said, "like right here, below that badge, man, so that it looked less like a badge and more like some, shit, light, when the knife went in."

I don't remember a great deal of the day-in, day-out from my youth, but I remember all of us—my mom included, until Lyme disease curled her quietly into a barely mobile, hardly audible echo—listening to Dad until we got bored even with his verve-ridden words about *pure life.* I do, though, remember him perking up with a reverence for his own dad which he surely held for no one else. Countless times Dad leaning, as he liked to do, against a wall, or laying on his back and looking up at the cracks on our ceiling, and telling us—with pearl eyes pleading we among this world of anonymity admit their worth—how it was, how this world really *was.* Men like his father killed on the job, their widows given a measly compensation "package." (He would cringe at the word package, the word sputtering repetitiously from his pursing lips like so many wads of spit.) *And yet we reward, babes, we reward them that don't do a damn thing for anyone but number one.*

When I was little I would press my ear against my parent's door almost every night, eager to catch whatever secrets demanded the door to be shut. In spite of all the spouts about *pure life,* if there was one word I heard more than any other it was *death.* Death.

"Enough," my mother said, "let's not do that again, okay?"

"Enough what? Don't you see what I mean? What if you were to die in a week? Don't tell me you'd be ready. Don't you want to *do* something with your life? Die a nameless nobody—that'd be okay with you? I don't believe it, Therese. What does it even mean to be 'ready,' to have 'lived a full life'?"

"WHAT does it mean, do you think, to have lived a full life?" I had asked Michelle earlier that night, swishing my wine around in an unintentional caricature of my question, waiting for her to complete the satire by saying something like "Live a full life, with Mount Blanc White Wines," remembering then that such were the niceties of the last time I had dated, some five years earlier, and that now there was less satisfaction to be drained from irony.

"That's a good one," she said, her fork now stabbing, with evident but not excess relish, the last piece of chicken covered in rich white sauce. "An easy one, of course," she said, her humor somehow more wholesome and less showy than what I was used to, able as she was to inhabit that landscape between deadening-gravity and everything-is-a-game. "If you'd asked me that three years ago, during my 'Western Buddhist' phase, I would have said something like, 'to be full is to be empty,' but come on, this sauce, this meal," she said, here proving her capacity to read the lines of my face, "is absolutely delicious and I'm not going to apologize for taking delight in it and getting full on it. But I'm talking about a full body..."—she had this way of parsing that clarified and cleansed even as it intoxicated the beholder—"and you asked about a full *life*. You want me to tell you the truth? Yes, of course you want me to. The truth is... and I know all the mechanisms and alarms that are going to go off in your head, but let them go on and on that's fine because the truth of the matter is that a *full* life now means a house filled with children scraping their knees and learning how to read, singing the songs I've taught them and learning how to give away the things they love the most."

I had hailed the waitress, and with outright indiscretion ordered another bottle of wine, one that cost the equivalent of diapers for twins for a month.

YEARS after he left, I learned that "full life," *pure life,* IT, or the same by any other name meant, for Dad, finishing what he had started, tasted, touched during doctoral work, the only "real" thing he had ever known. My parents met in graduate school, which my mother later came to call "indoctrination," and into which my father threw himself as one does from the fire escape of a burning building into the arms of professors who hardly knew how to catch him. He leaped with a ruinous leap from which he never fully recovered, as though the part of him that dealt with friends and family came out crippled and left only a monomaniacal muscle straining after the search. While my mother dropped out to use her social work degree in a government services program that provided food and nutrition education to pregnant women, my father climbed the ladders of praise that his professors tilted dizzyingly up. Phrases like "the grammar of social structures" became to mother the stuff of well-intentioned jokes, but these my father felt as jabs, and many of our family dinners shifted from these seemingly thoughtless jests into a silence that held our heads down, leaving us nearly drowning in the bowls of soup laid out before us. In uninterrupted silence we chewed our peas and meat, and I always thought of those dinners when a noir film came on the television, during the part where the gunman tells everyone to shut up.

And then the music arrives on stage, unseen but there. Helping you to feel.

My father's dissertation, which he never completed, was to use some ideas of the philosopher Wittgenstein to analyze—he wanted to bridge philosophy with everydayness—the language of clerks in convenience stores. He never completed it. My sister Marguerite was born before he finished the second chapter.

"What we cannot speak about we must consign to silence," my father repeated, during an upswing, when dinners involved full wine glasses for Mom and Dad and a stunning orange sparkling grapefruit drink for Marguerite and me.

"Let me guess? Wittgenstein," my mother said, touching her curled hair, which sprung back up after she pulled it down around her neck, sad-eyed still even though this upswing brought old spring dresses out of the closet, shook off and spread open Brontë's *Wuthering Heights* from its near-death on a dusty bookshelf, and in her prayers a dash of praise alongside beseechings that always trailed off into no words at all.

What we cannot speak about we must consign to silence.

During the downswings, Dad would leave the house without a slam, would nestle the door closed as though in so doing he could keep his exit secret. I stacked three cardboard boxes into a flimsy tower that lasted just long enough for me to see him there, pacing the backyard as though it were a foreign land, holding his own hands behind his back with something clenched there—a notebook, a knife, a map, the hem of *pure life?*—walking with a brisk step that made my eyes hurt as I tried to follow him through the blinds which I barely dared to slit open.

What we cannot speak about we must consign to sight.

"God," I said. "Can you do something?" Mom and Dad did not talk about God but Grandma did, and, especially when for six months that may as well have been years, filled as they were with jokes made of kneaded puns and fresh bread she let us help her bake, Dad went to work in a chemical factory an hour outside of the city. There he worked packaging and loading Botox product displays that shipped out to malls and hotel conferences and the like, even as Mom continued to feed pregnant and nursing mothers with sometimes only canned green beans blanched of anything that would give them the dignified name *food*, other times fresh cilantro and onions and giant cloves of garlic, which she would describe to us with V-armed rapture. During this stretch we were at Grandma's most days, sitting on the orange couch with yellow stripes that felt like an approachable sun, warm and bright, staring out of her big bay window at the cars, chilled with simultaneous sorrow and delight whenever Mom came to pick us up and take us home. Dad would come home smelling like the lemon and vinegar admixture we used to disinfect the bathroom, except you could tell that the lemon scent was fake.

And he would kiss us so long as we were asleep. I would pretend to be deep in dreams whenever I heard his heavy factory boots growing closer. So long as I was asleep, he would hold me like that lost life, like I myself may well have been that *pure life*, balled up there, on the creaky bed. He'd cradle my head in one palm and brush my cheek with his wet nose. I did not wipe the wetness off, not even long after he left and I lay there tingling with something I could not name.

I TURNED from Dad, looked back at our table, and perfectly-dim as the place was, I spotted first Michelle's teeth, which almost glowed (she admitted, when I once made an off-handed comment, that she had started brushing with coconut oil and turmeric before she posted her profile picture to the dating website, one more thing I found refreshing: she was not vain, but also not quietly self-conscious). How potent a little unpretentious fashion can be. Again tonight she wore the mint-colored dress with the purple scarf that she braided and circled her neck in the shape of a wildflower's into a bounteous bloom. Over the past few months I found myself doing silly things like envying the coffee cups on which her lipstick left prints. With her the kiss became the *aim*, knowing as I did that in her mind sex was forbidden before vows. Somehow, I found myself grateful that none of this would end with a bedsheet tangle. And then, you see, she had this look, an alternation of direct glances that felt like dilating eye drops in your own, and sidelong gazes that burned with her concern for something larger than you and larger than this room, or the deepest troubles of our times—real as these were to her—something not only larger than this world and all within it but more pure: all of which meant that not everything hung on whether this date and the next ones would work out or not, or even whether her life at its end would add up to little more than a collage of failures. You can find a counterfeit of this gaze in certain young people who inhale the promises of God in the manner a *flâneur* does his opium, their glazed-over eyes promising detachment from anything that could make claims on them.

MY father turned to me not like a father to his son but as to a friend with whom one has shared fierce loyalty. His mouth had evened out some, so that the permanent smile did not sneak out like a secret, and I couldn't help feeling bad for him; it was clear that somewhere along the way that privileged line to the divine with which he had won over even the hardest unbeliever had snapped, just as the line of children had tripped him in his tracks all those years back. But what was it? What bull, what minotaur had managed to leave the champion defeated?

"How did IT—" I tried to ask.

"IT didn't," he said, rubbing his standard fit Dickies with one hand and pulling at his nose with the other, something like giving the finger to any claims that he might be lying, a yellow-edged copy of Wittgenstein sticking out of his pocket, tucked alongside a notebook. "It just took me longer than it should have to see the simple truth. It's possible for *whole lives* to be consigned to silence. And that's something I'd not been ready to swallow, all those years ago." He held out his hands, showing them almost purple and pruned, and whispered with gravity, "This my mean task, would be as heavy to me as odious, but the mistress which I serve quickens what's dead and makes my labors pleasures."

And there it was. The gleam returned with such force that I couldn't decide if he had perfected the role of conjuring puppeteer (thereby ever-deferring the need to say those horrendous words *I was wrong*). But then something else crept around the gleam: the stretch of eyelid skin that spells out guilt, eyelids that, ever so slowly, snuffed out the gleam entirely.

"If you haven't noticed it," he said, trying to push up his eyelids, his eyes big marbles again, knocking all the others out of the unseen circle that surrounded him and winning, winning, winning: "All the Titanics are sinking, babe," he said, signaling to a co-worker, who obeyed immediately, taking my father's position at the dish line, the dishes like so many dirty vessels waiting to be ferried from the infernal shores through the machine that would make them pure again. "Listen now to this," he said, in that tone that made first-time hearers double-take, thinking he was drunk, which was part of the magic: no substance drove this *pure life.* "Talking to this boy about your age," he said, as though I were still fifteen and not thirty, "Oxford, o ye great Oxford University, seat of the long-gone-dons, so long. Oxford's own university press, boy, they done it with this new children's dictionary, he says. Done away with a whole world of words that spelled something great: altar, chapel, monastery, nun, psalm, monk, devil, saint. Sure as the sun rise doing it again every damn day, they did away with all these old great words and switched a whole new slew of them: vandalism and negotiate, committee and bullet point. Son of a bitch—I ain't lying, boy. Here's the kicker. Monarch was dethroned, decapitated, culled under the cover and darkness and replaced by this one: celebrity." Here he walked backward and grabbed a knife off the butcher block, set it to his heart like that addict had to his father's, did so in such a way that it seemed another man's hand, not his, held it there, and said, "This age's no place for us, boy. Celebrities sucking the royal blood out of the world." He thrust out his chest, proclaimed:

> "Our enemies have beat us to the pit:
> It is more worthy to leap in ourselves,
> Than tarry till they push us."

He pulled out a red-covered spiral notebook about the size of his hand, flipped through some fifty pages of scrawl, and read, "'by averageness and leveling down, everything gets obscured, and what has thus been covered up gets passed off as something familiar and accessible to everyone . . . by virtue of an insensitivity to all distinctions in level and genuineness, and in providing average intelligibility, opens up a standard world in which all distinctions between the unique and the general, the superior and the average, the important and the trivial have been leveled.' *Being and Time,* babe," he said, "the damned fool Heidegger hits it again," here his voice rising as he bangs a hanging pan that resounds like a bell, capturing me with the look of knowing that only those who have known you in diapers can render.

"But—"

"Now don't get me wrong. Lived the life of a fucking bastard messenger who knew for damn sure we were meant for something GREAT—touching you young'uns with lightning and then, feeling the charge go out of myself and into you I… I saw what it'd do. What it did," and here we were walking toward the back of the backroom, his hand pulling my collar in a manner both friendly and commanding, his other hand holding out the red notebook, letting it fall to the floor with a mournful release, fingers outstretched then not in rejection of the words he'd copied into it but, I wondered, as his eyes searched me for a long second, but in something like repentance. For he dropped it as though it were the pressed, bleached, and bound once-branches of the tree of the knowledge of good and evil, tucked for too long into his back pocket.

"What it did to your mother," he said, suddenly tight-lipped, squinting hard at what stars showed themselves as we went out into the wet night of Eugene, Oregon, a wetness that, when we were young and left by him with our bed-ridden mother, would dampen the skin so deeply that it would force the five of us together into one bed, our bodies a furnace.

"Lyme, Dad, it was *Lyme,* not *kids* that did Mom in." That did it. When I said *Dad* I exorcised the indifference right out of his body, so that his hand, still holding the knife borrowed to pick up where the power of language and charisma left off, shook. "Dad. Dad. Dad," I said, rhythmically, as though pressing the word down on his chest, as though breathing it into his mouth the way I had learned to practice CPR on a mannequin.

"They don't want a leader," he said, leaning against the large green trash receptacle that towered over him and made him small. "This age. They don't want a leader even in making everything average and equal and all they want, you see, you see, cause that would *defeat the whole thing—to have a leader that would lead them into equality would do away with the blessed equality,*" he

said, getting this last claim out quickly, as feeling the immuniza-
tion that had kept him above everything sapped and sucked from
him every time I called him by that name.

"Dad," I said, bizarrely composed. "But," and here I coughed
up the composure already, unseeing him suddenly, seeing only a
light in such stark contrast to the scene that surrounded him that
its eeriness went like an ice pick into the temple, "have you, have
you seen Mom?"

"Why do you think they leak every embarrassing scrap from
the past of everyone that rises? *Leveling*," he said

"Dad."

"Leveling."

"Daddy," I said, and his left knee lost its lock, went lax and
left him struggling to find balance.

"Baby breath," he said, his voice pure cane sugar, curing the
ache that swelled around my eye at once. "Baby breath," he said,
talking not now to me but to my mother, turned even in the
direction of her apartment as though he knew all along and in
spite of it never dropped her dime, a dram, or a damn's worth of
his time, gave her less uplift than a willow bent under an Oregon
storm.

"You know if she's still *here?*" he asked, not pointing anywhere, meaning, I presumed, *still not dead,* or, *still in existence,* or
however he might have articulated it, any remaining steadiness
interrupted by the pubescent crack of his own indomitable voice.

I nodded.

"Baby breath," he said. "Baby breath."

I SAW the table he had set for her when I was four, a table made
of taped-together cardboard after we had moved into a new
apartment and broken the legs of our Duncan Phyfe beyond
repair. The cardboard he had covered with a tapestry of royal
purple, so that the baby's breath he laid there reached out like
the neck of a medieval queen, lifting upward until it bloomed in a

head of dandelions, weeds he had somehow arranged into flowers, golden bloom to white wish to death breath, golden bloom to white wish to death breath set before our mother when she came home from the doctor that day, her Lyme diagnosis POSITIVE emboldened on the page of charts and symbols otherwise signifying to us nothing. After she had phoned with the results he insisted she head over to her sisters, which I've no doubt she assumed meant he was admitting his own inability to do or say what was right and sparing her the inevitable disappointment.

But he suspended his usual incredible aloofness, completed a frenzy of internet research, ten minutes later emerging from the little closet office with a scrawled recipe. Another ten minutes and he had returned from the co-op down the street, sent us outside, and went to work. Through the window, wafts of rarefied delight pulled our noses toward the ledge, peeking in to see the kitchen table and sink splattered with batter the size of rice grains, spoons and spatulas scattered every which way in a frenzy of—joy. Dad was humming the song that had played at their wedding, which we had heard in the homespun wedding video several times late one night, when Mom watched it on repeat with no explanation some years ago. When Mom walked through the front door he called us through the back, though we were already at the threshold, ready to rush through the door.

Her high heels. She never wore them, but somehow a trip to the doctor drew them out of the closet. The click clack had the rhythm of iambic pentameter, and between the steps you could hear her blowing her nose, so lightly, so lightly into the handkerchief she had sewn when she was a child.

"Baby breath," he said, pointing at the vase of baby's breath and dandelions, letting her eyes open and close at the sight of something so atypical and impossible to categorize that it could only register as some sort of mystery. Out of the oven then he pulled the cake, saying "coconut, a really good anti-fungal and anti-microbial, lemon, stimulate your liver without doing you in,

I gutted and squeezed about four of them, and cilantro, just a spoonful, superb for removing toxins, and, yes rice flour, and just three strawberries crushed and spread throughout the batter."

The cake glowed, a candle in the middle casting constellations of light through its sides, and my mother, when she saw it, snatched it out at once, then gathered her nerves just as quickly before she turned to him and said, "It's my baptismal candle."

"It was the only one I could find."

"You must have looked through the whole house, the whole closet then," she said, seeing his eyes droop satisfactorily the way a dog does when it knows it's being praised.

"Smells like lemon," my brother Sammy said, eyes ignited with delight. "And this time not cause you're cleaning the toilet, Da."

"Your mother needs something strong to clean out her insides," Dad said, gesturing to her as only he could do, so that she seemed both a mannequin in need of CPR-revival and the object of his love, perhaps never more before than at that hour. "Your mother is sick," he said. "But we will clean that bug right out of her. It's just a matter of time."

And she *moved* into him, so that he had to balance the cake on one arm while she almost *fell* into him, with all of that weight, and I saw him hold her, stay steady with her heave. Saw. It. All. Happen. So. Slow. And I smiled with a brightness that could out-clean any lemon, and he held her, and then she held him, as he set the cake down on the table, scooped a piece out with his fingers, and put it right in her mouth while Sammy and I filled our faces with the rest, while her mouth found his and rested there.

That was the last time they kissed. He was out the door not long after, mumbling something about his leaving making it easier for her to get state aid.

WHEN we arrived at Mom's apartment I took my hand out of my pocket to punch the code I'd memorized from weekends dropping off groceries and reading her bits of the newspaper and the Book of Revelation at her request. Dad cut me off, entering it himself, keeping a straight face as though to keep me in suspense, staying silent, back turned to me and hands folded awkwardly in the elevator as we ascended, passing the various layers of this purgatorial high rise, arriving at last at her state-subsidized one-bedroom.

Mom's eyes crossed at first when we both walked through the door, as though she were trying to hold us both in the same gaze and failed. She shifted slightly in her bed and my eyes fixated on the tremble, visible only if you focused hard, visible at the edges of her head, a tremble that cut an aureole into the pillow. She lifted both of her hands and pulled us toward her with unseen strings.

"Babe," Dad said, "I found the prodigal," resting his elbow on my shoulder and messing up my hair.

"I think *I* did," she said, pointing at Dad with the one working eye, the one that the Lyme had not done in over time. "Though I wasn't ready to tell him you've been coming. I was waiting to see if you'd stick," she said, eking each word out only with great effort, her chest heaving at the end under an old afghan that used to cover the orange couch at Grandma's. So warm.

"Those who can't stick must be consigned to silence," he said. "And I'm… mmm. Wouldn't rather be stuck any elsewhere, babe. Here," he said. "With you. In this silence," he said. And we stayed there long into the night, saying almost nothing, stayed there as though stuck, as though we had climbed into her room and had thrown away the ladder.

BUT I'm sorry. Back to Michelle.

My father kissed Michelle at the end of the aisle, the guilty stretch and sag of his eyelids wiped out by the gleam in her own. There she stood, my wife, at the other end of that same aisle over which the priest splattered holy water, the teardrops of God beating against Mom's coffin in the almost empty church.

Heavyweight

TIGHT-WRAPPED in white blankets, the children were coated with that uncommon consolation of silence, one in the claustrophobic crib that Jimmy himself had slept in when he was a baby and the other in the pulled-out dresser drawer propped up by sleeves of baseball cards collected in childhood. A friend of the family had recommended this method on accident. She had said that when her husband was in medical school and their family was young they had no money for cribs so they pulled out the dresser drawer and it worked—although they had used copies of *The Wall Street Journal* instead. Yes, they drew some looks from visitors and even some vinegar words, but you know in the end it all worked out. It all would work out, the friend of the family had told Katie, this when Jimmy was still deployed, this with arms full of a lasagna pan crisscrossed with two massive Italian forearms of bread loaves. It did not work. When she said that. The words worked on Katie like medicine that could have been helpful in a smaller dose but which she could barely swallow then. She could not consider what she would have done if he had not been discharged.

Katie sat there across from Jimmy. She always did that: sat across from him so that they would not start out together but would have to move toward melding at some point. So that at some point, if both children remained horizontal and hushed, Katie and Jimmy would perhaps lay across the long couch that she had in fact started laboring on when their youngest—the infant in the padded dresser drawer, packed in there, small in there so there was no way at he could slip out—started making his way into the world. Katie made her eyes into slits and peeled apart the blinds, leaning toward the frozen window.

"What?" Jimmy asked. "Who is it?"

"Shh," she said, and, still propping the blinds apart with two fingers, she swung her other hand around and, finding the light switch, turned it until their living room blacked out. "Come here," she said. He heard the couch springs complain. But it was not the couch springs that complained. When their twang finished he heard another noise seeping in through the window's thin cracks left by architect or builder.

"Who is it?" Jimmy asked, tangling his body with hers. That was something she never failed to like. The days since he'd been back from the war had been entirely cold. The desert had been perpetual sand in swarms in the closest thing he'd ever felt to that word *eternal*. The uneasy eternality of endlessness. It was of course in time because it ended, but things like that can put you in a mind to really consider it: heaven, or, in this case, hell. He hadn't killed anyone, although on a few missions he had shot in a surefire way and with a confidence reminiscent of Cassius Clay's before the match with Sonny Liston. Someone had to fail, though. Someone had to lose. It was all part of the game. But these thoughts—thoughts spurred from the fact that, according to the rules, someone had to lose the game—began to make his right hand shake, in the mess hall, as he tried to shovel dinner onto his hungry tongue. And he was on leave now after a medical assessment of the mental sort.

They only let him leave therapy after he stopped repeating, "It's all a game" to every question asked, using "It's all a game" to cut off every conversation.

Katie peered out the window. She breathed through a small hole on the left side of her mouth so her exhalations did not fog the view. And now Jimmy saw. Tangled up with her legs, his arm around her waist, he saw the man shouting and swinging something in the hail. Earlier it had been snow and even for a time rain but with night the sky hatched these little pellets of hail from on high.

No matter how hard they tried they could not keep their breath enough away from the window. Every few minutes the man was obscured. The storm's rumbling and its precipitation—which came down in lines like the dotted outline of a blueprint for many church spires that reached up from the city—already obscured most of the action. So it was good after all that they had failed to secure the storm windows. It was good that they could open the inner glass and listen and see better through the screen, holding one another closer both for warmth and because of what they heard which was *I'll kill you I swear to God I'll kill you if you don't stop dealing man I swear it talk to someone who knows me I live up to my word man there's kids in this neighborhood man and you bringing in these punks all day to get high in the back seat of your car don't think I don't know I'm sick of you living off of everybody else man I'm done with it this has to stop I'll hit your head into left field you sonofabitch I's number one in home runs on my block when I's a kid*, screaming and swinging something that looked like and yes it was clear now it was an baseball bat.

And then Katie put it all together almost as soon as the window was lifted almost as soon as the chill sobered them up and stole any romance from their stance there on the couch because the man was standing in front of the house of Vic who fixed cars officially if illegally all day long he fixed cars out there on the street and his hands were entirely blackened by grease but something else passed through those hands also and everyone knew it and even the cops tried to stake out the house but by some awful luck or something they could never catch him with the actual sacks of white powder in his hands, circular sacks that looked like baseballs ready to be passed from hand to hand before some bat came to swing them over the fence as if it was all part of the game.

Soon he was swinging not just at the empty air but at the

base of an old oak that towered naked some twenty feet up into the sky and you could hear his teeth crack against one another just after he delivered his blows to the base of the tree in a skillful manner that was impressive for its sheer ingenuity because the tree when it fell would land on top of Vic's house. And it did. *My name is Thomas Angler* the man said, as he pushed his lower back against the hollowed out wedge of the tree, as though hankering after some immortality, as though eventually the tree itself would timber and he would use the thing itself as a bat with which to beat the other team. Jimmy's head swam with these thoughts, and his right hand started shaking again, so he held it under his bent knee before Katie could see. Tired of those medications.

My name is Thomas Angler you come out now and fight me like a man Vic you step up to a man's challenge now Vic I got two ways about it Vic you either come at me bare fisted in this street here or you let me hit them bags of coke over the fence, and if I hit three homeruns in a row you got to take your business out a this neighborhood. Your choice. Those two or I'll drop this thing on your house man, this bat won't break I swear it can take anything, even this tree.

And they said very little Katie and Jimmy, because Katie too now knew the source of that trembling she felt, the reason her husband's hand was hidden and shaking, for she had been there at those therapy sessions when he repeated "It's only a game," said this even about their marriage, said that in a marriage someone always wins and someone always loses, with a voluminous intensity that contrasted absolutely their present silence, as they watched with a shared terror and glee and just as at last Jimmy asked "You think we should call the police? This isn't a game. I mean, someone could get killed," at which her eyes whetted just slightly. Just as at last they lifted the phone out and moved beyond the pure purview of spectators into the mode of guilt for having taken it all in at the expense of reality which was the tree falling on Vic's house with a crack like the collapse of a rebel stronghold in the desert but somehow more so like the slap of a hand against face and it is the hand of a superior officer against his subordinate after the diplomacy and rhetorical weave of an argument snapped into that force which does not die as easily as words because words can always be reinterpreted and the more awful meaning massaged out so that all you have left is an ambiguous symbol and the terrible language games, but there was nothing ambiguous or symbolic about the tree collapsing on Vic's house and coming within an inch of his head.

VIC did stop dealing. Or at least he moved away. Because the tree had come within an inch of his head and had not in fact crushed his skull, as witnessed by Katie and Jimmy and the neighborhood *en masse*, the faces that stared like salivating spectators at a match, stared fixedly from attics and turrets and windows with iron bars over them and windows buttressed by red silk curtains made by hand. They all remembered that night with some laughs, though they were thin and tenuous and awful laughs that left knots in the stomach, knots that amateur boxers get by simply looking at opponents, knots that could not be undone by antacid tablets or ginger ale drinks. And from time to time they'd laugh until a small column of the newspaper, few words and miniscule print, announced his name. Not the way he would have wanted it. Not in the sports section with a byline reading *Wins Again*. Not that way. No. The axe man's obituary story did not read like everyone else. It did not say Thomas was survived by so-and-so, or that he would be fondly missed by these people, that he held the home run record of the Clear Creek neighborhood baseball league. Instead, it was an odd blend of some outside voice and the very words of the suicide note. Before the multiple sclerosis set in, it said, and he lived under the care of his uncle and, the obituary took pains to emphasize, *I cannot make it clear enough how grateful I am for the people of this country who paid for my disability services even those who did so begrudgingly, even those who might consider me a lazy bum feeding off their hard work.* Before the multiple sclerosis, the third person voice resumed, Thomas Angler had been a promising boxer in a dying sport and he'd always said he was born too late he was made for the days of Sonny Liston, who weighed in without flinching as Cassius Clay gave his guttural "I'm ready to rumble... I'm the champ," who listened to these taunts as a beekeeper listens to the buzzing of bees, with perfect serenity. Those were the days when games had dignity. He'd even written some articles on boxing for sporting and popular interest magazines, articles in which he argued that every culture needs a more or less violent sport, somewhat vicious games, if it does not want to have its population constantly at war or constantly taking aim at the wrong targets.

Jimmy read these articles alone, unable to sleep one night. As the sun rose he stuffed an old coarse coffee bean bag with pennies and tissue, feeling the outside before he punched it to make sure the outer interior was soft, so that his knuckles would not break or something. He tightened a wheat-colored piece of braided rope around the mouth of the sack and pulled tight. Then he removed the dangling light fixture in the middle of the living room, the one they never used anyhow because the wires were too old for comfort. He tied the empty end of the rope to a nub that was all that remained of the once useless and dangling dome of light. He stood back and stared at it hanging there, swinging back and forth there deadly. And he punched it. He hit that dead weight until his knuckles bled, then washed his hands as priests do, at the altar, before they consecrate the holy sacrifice of the Mass. He had been an altar server. He remembered the way they washed their hands ceremoniously so that the people could get a good sense of how dirty we can be and how badly we need to be cleaned and that was one sure thing about hitting that stuffed coffee bean bag he knew first-hand the horrors that lived inside him somewhere waiting to be squeezed or exorcized out or what have you. He knew then something of what Thomas Angler meant in his article "Boxing: A Religious Ritual." What he meant was that we will sacrifice somebody or something, it is just a matter of what or whom, and it was a matter of organizing the sacrifice and ordering the violence, and after the sacrifice, when the game ended, it was a question of whether the crowd would gravitate toward the winner, and ride his triumphal rise, or cling to the loser, and even sometimes deify him for embodying that thing—failure—which is all too easy to worship. Jimmy thought, his head throbbing with adrenaline, excitement, horror as he came to it, and—. He couldn't quite piece it together. No. But there was no need to do so. Or, he was suspicious of his impulse to do so. Instead, he tried to let the vision of the dangling makeshift punching bag overtake the uninvited image of Thomas Angler hanging likewise from an attic ceiling as he headed to the shower and let the cold water pelt him like the hail that had pummeled the man through the blinds that big deal night. I'm sorry, he said, in his head. Then, "I'm sorry," aloud, "I should have played with you… should have let you win… no, should have told somebody about the real win you scored, that night, when you beat Vic, oh God," allowing the water to run into his mouth until he gagged and spat it out like a boxer mid-match, returning from the corner of the ring. "I'm sorry."

The Man Watching

I mean the Angel who appeared
to the wrestlers of the Old Testament:
when the wrestlers' sinews
grew long like metal strings,
he felt them under his fingers
like chords of deep music.

Whoever was beaten by this Angel
(who often simply declined the fight)
went away proud and strengthened
and great from that harsh hand
that kneaded him as if to change his shape.
Winning does not tempt that man.

—"The Man Watching," Rainer Maria Rilke

"IT'S *craysczy*," he said, standing on the other side of the brand-new chain-link fence the landlord installed to keep the pit bulls out, snorting and hacking up some spit, hurling it like a comet in an incredible arc across the grass, which in the drought had gone the golden color of ripe wheat. What was *craysczy* was that they were now bombing hospitals and elementary schools. "*Craysczy* men. More than a million from there are now another me, refugees," he said. He gripped the glass column in his hand and cranked the handle and crushed more pepper onto the slices of potato laid in think circles across the open grill, then laughed. "Look at this man why we had to leave." He turned some of the smokier potatoes and leaned against the chain link fence between us. Lifted up his khaki short the color of dry green grass, and, unsatisfied, rolled it up and set his heel on top of a tree stump so that I could see the lightning-zig-zag of a scar that shot across the socket of his thigh. "Look at this."

"My God," I said.

"Man," he said, "you read books like this waiter I work with when I showed him this one he called me Jacob. Do you know what he means *Jacob*? Do you know that story?" Mohammed asked, rotating his still-red scar even as he turned the shish kebab on the grill, so that the red caught the sun and shined a little even.

"I don't know what he means," I said.

"Have you *wrestled* with God?" he asked.

"Have you?" I asked, the question barely escaping my constricted throat.

He turned around and scraped the potatoes now completely coated in brown but not burnt onto a china-blue plate that he balanced now on top of the shaving horse he used to build things. He shook his head *no* and then *yes,* then let go of a heavy breath as he stared into the coals under the grill.

Back in Lebanon he was a carpenter and would be still except for the terrible bodily aches that get bad even as a dishwasher but would be too bad to bear if he were to do what he used to do on ladders or bent over all day long. "The pain killers barely work," he told me some days before, and then his wife told my wife he was addicted. I hung my head because he had no way to see a doctor without going into debt and I tried to broach the subject but he told me he was doing well and smiled with his big teeth that said he could take it, that said he's been through enough and hinted at the scar he now held up and said "Shrapnel."

"God," he said. "Ha." Then, pointing at the scar, tracing it with the tongs he was using to flip lamb, he said "Some kid. Some homemade grenade he threw at me. I thought it was a rock at first I don't know what I was thinking. It was at the beginning of the civil war and he was Muslim and you see I had my name changed to Mohammed then because I had a Muslim friend who was with the Palestinians who took over at the beginning of the civil war and he had one made for me a new I.D. card that listed me as Muslim. You know that at the beginning they could go around and check our I.D. cards and the Christians they would kill on the spot and then not too long later the Christians did the same thing to the Muslims."

The day was draining out now and the large orange light from inside my apartment started to hit Mo's forehead. Mo stood there, basked in the echoes of orange light, and said his family's Visas were expiring and the lawyer at the immigration office was not saying nice things like he used to and if nothing else happened their family would be back in Lebanon.

"You know what that would mean?" he asked me, as though I were willfully ignorant, which I was. "Do you know what it is like to *wrestle* with God?" he asked me as though there was no such thing as news as though only he had access to what was happening from talking with his mother who still ran the family store in Beirut.

"You know that the Syrian war is now in Lebanon how you say *spilling* over into Lebanon. I look at those schools they bomb and those children's caskets did you see he?" he asked with something wet, some pinpoints of wet speckling his face even as now he laughed a little and chewed a rough potato piece then spat it out, the steam still visible as it lay cooling on the grass.

"When I was there we broke Albulena's leg trying to fit her into the back sack the thing on our back. We broke her leg. She was one year old something then but had to because the back sack was small and we had so much miles to walk she held onto the icon my wife—religious—made Albulena carry the Michael the Archangel her greatmother no her grandmother gave us made by some Marionite monk. I swear to God I didn't mean to when I said 'God should stick to having his angels put their swords into the devils and leave us alone.' I didn't know what I was saying and didn't know what I was saying when I yelled the same at the waiter and now one more job lost. Boss says he can't have me harassing his employees. God," he said, running his finger across the scar, first roughly and then with the firm care of a harp-player plucking the deepest string. But though I almost heard the chord, for the first time I suspected something like rancor in the clench of his smiling teeth.

NOW I know that rancor did not tempt Mohammed, that the rancor was mine. Mine against the dominions under whom is not made dumb as we lean there on the fence, me leaning away a little like a child testing gravity, dizzied a little by his wound and what it meant, squinting until he blurred and the light made him luminous around the edges and my God, I asked, *what is your name?* And still from this our exile I ask *tell me your name,* and when I do the rancor lifts like smoke from the hot ashes.

Gates of Eden

The motorcycle black madonna
Two-wheeled gypsy queen
And her silver-studded phantom cause
The gray flannel dwarf to scream
As he weeps to wicked birds of prey
Who pick up on his bread crumb sins
And there are no sins inside the Gates of Eden
—Bob Dylan, "Gates of Eden"

AFTER SEVEN CITY COUNCIL meetings, a run of political cartoons in the local paper that featured the mayor now tarred and
now feathered, now inside and now outside of a wiry coop, they
finally made them legal. Chickens in the backyard. For most this
meant either instant indifference or the run-of-the-mill intoxica-
tion of novelty, complete with designer chicken cages that ranged
from two to four thousand dollars. For a smaller minority it
came as a smoky whiff of some embodiment of pure Emerson
self-reliance or one small step toward *going back to the land*—all of
these ideas incarnate in a dream of three or four fresh-laid eggs
per day, eggs the hand could reach for and touch still warm, hot
even, not chilled and stacked by the thousands in the supermarket. But for Abdul it meant food. Necessity.

Waiting for the ovals hatched each morning and protected by
the hens until his hand would stick a twig to her rear—to displace
her and then thieve them. They were always smaller than his
stomach. He endured these little contributions the way a landlord

endures the petty rent of a favorite tenant who has lost his job but still, being human, requires at the very least a roof and a bed, and so, compassionate as he is, the landlord allows him to occupy an undesirable studio on the topmost floor (but the toilet works and there is a small sink and stove) in exchange for his sweeping the hallways weekly and offering up on the doormat of the landlord a few canned goods bought with his food stamps, all the while both knowing this charity will demand the now delayed but inevitable reckoning.

This morning, already at six thirty, Abdul's patience had been rotted out by a strange dream of a chicken leg marinated in seven secret spices and turned on a spit for an hour above just enough coals to cook it but not so many that a black coating of char would crop up, all at once, the chicken leg dancing as though on stage in front of him, denying him. By chance, today, when he peeks in through the hen house made from scrap oak and shoddy nails with a carpenter's eyes that can measure to the centimeter how large she is, he sees that she is large enough. And today, a national holiday of some sort, although he knows not what precisely is being celebrated, any onlooking neighbors (men in lawn chairs, women on second-story porches, children settling into spots on top of recently-scaled garages) can see his left hand tight around the wet and feathery bone just behind the beak, right knee planted oblong from the breast to the base of the bird's body, right hand training the blade on that choice stretch of neck most agreeable to the coming snap.

Abdul's whole body knows how to move in such a way that, his hand gripped around the throat-end of the axe, a single graceful swing—not unlike some baseball great doing the job at the first pitch—will finish her off with hardly a foul sound, a sound hardly as hard to hear as the wife in the apartment beside theirs at night, the *don't hurt me, don't hurt me,* heard on the hottest nights when there was no choice between shutting the windows and dealing with the stuffiness and keeping them open and keeping cool but having to hear her cries again. Abdul had called the police once, although it was against his every nerve to involve *them*. That night he had choked his suspicion of them, his fury over time after time being detained at airports, and he dialed. By the time they arrived the father was finished, and before the officer could even mount the several staircases to the third floor the father had lined up his whole family in front of the apartment, the one sided hastily once by Abdul's cousin Sammy, whose bid was accepted because it was at least half the cost of any of the others, the one whose yellow siding was undressing itself awkwardly now, its yellow shingles falling in coughs of plaster dust even as the father's three children and his dull-eyed wife said, *No officer I don't know who could have thought that; everything is alright.*

ABDUL'S teeth are noticeably large. He is happy. He has just snapped the chicken's head off and now, between decapitation and defeathering, he holds the neck of a green beer bottle like the axe he swung in a single motion, draining nearly half of it in one drink. He leans his large arms against the fence, arms covered in small splotches of mossy hair, the fence divides him from Blaise, who too laid awake the night Abdul called the police at the fifth *don't hurt me, don't hurt me,* who instead of calling the police had in his mind hurdled the white picket that blocked out the alley and in one bound arrived before the apartment door, hearing the archetypal wrestle inside, axe in pocket, then in hand, then the dream's impotence is admitted, because there is only one axe in the apartment complex, and it is Abdul's. The fence is tall with extended rows of links installed to cage the German Shepherd that moved into the house planted square in the middle of the backyard, planted there when the Polish immigrants first brought over their whole families. The dog that last week leaped over the fence's old height and tore flesh from the ankle of Blaise's baby. The fence extension hangs at a thirty degree angle from the original, and it is only missing barbwire for the feeling *this is a godforsaken prison, we live in a godforsaken prison* that surges like a wild animal into Blaise's brain each time he passes it, to be too accurate.

Today he leans against it, looks at Abdul, and their eyes catch in a flitting omniscience that says, *we will not be here forever, in* this, *we will not live here forever... will we?* Abdul is tenant to his cousin Sammy the landlord who has again in hard times allowed an old friend to inhabit the condemned building in the backyard, the building without power except that coming from an orange cord run through Sammy's attic, the building that has become some kind of revolving door for God only knows. When Blaise or even Abdul ask questions or sneak flashes of disapproval in front of Sammy—because with Sammy, who always smiles, there is no confrontation, there is only the chance that some subtle incongruous grin or some seemingly accidental admission will result in Sammy taking action some days later, as though he does so only on his own volition and inspiration—he acts as though nothing has been said, as though there is no man living there, as though the man who lives there has no tremors of withdrawal, as though the dog either does not exist or is not fierce enough to steal the flesh—albeit a barely noticeable scrape of cells; it was the act more than the actual amount of skin stolen that shocked—of an infant.

But today the dog was asleep or ranging the basement of that godforsaken backyard house, was nowhere near the decapitated chicken, growling and drooling in expectation. Blaise leaned over the fence, nodded at the half de-feathered thing, made weak humming noises that seemed desperate to signify satisfaction and said, his eyes fixed on the new queen hen's nervous neck, "I have to say, I admire your abilities."

"I can deliver your wife's baby, too, if you like," Abdul offered. "Could. In Lebanon. Here I am... There are many other *abilities* I have that I cannot use here. That are good for nothing here." Abdul's wife Albuelena had told Blaise's wife Sophia that in Lebanon, where they were from, at least in the part they lived, it was common for the husband to do the delivery.

THEY first moved to the United States on student visas. An admissions counselor advised a smiling and sweating Abdul as to the best loan rates and helped him pick out classes characteristic for a first year pre-medical student. Abdul was then thirty. By thirty-one he had learned enough English to make a grade higher than the Ds that lined the computer screen like sideways smirks at semester's end. Albuelena, who, having worked in her father's hotel, better heard and spoke the English language, studied business. And the children, Mariette, 2, and Paul, 1, when they first settled into Mill City, went several days per week to a daycare run by three nuns in their seventies and staffed by single mothers who watched their own children while they brought in enough to live on. The nuns offered three charity clients at a time, and Albuelena, who had worked for four weeks to fill out the three-page application essay, won them these silent hours of scrambled studying and awkward fights that less and less now, around the time of the chickens, ended in an "I'm leaving," and an adjoining, "Where will you go? There is nowhere for you to go." Once they even laughed and congratulated themselves for being able to fight in English.

It was temporary, the arrangement. Abdul said this each time the student loan statement came in the mail. At the base of the loan statement in big capital letters it said: THIS IS NOT A BILL.

"This life is temporary," Albuelena said, at last, after three years of the same, around the time of the chickens, whose presence had helped her to sigh a little with a certain settled feeling.

Abdul passed the student loan statement over the fence, and asked Blaise to hold it.

"I got a contracting job. Doing roofs. This will be done with," he said, lifting the axe and cutting the statement in two. The blade, still bloodied, left stains on the two halves of the statement, which fluttered in a gust of wind and disappeared over the top of the apartment complex. Abdul's eyes followed them and then landed on the spire of Our Lady of Divine Providence church that towered above the coops and the dirty bowling alleys of the bohemian neighborhood. "Come," he said, dropping the ax and turning on the hose, rinsing his hands and then drying then in the grass. "I'll show you which roof I will be on."

Blaise followed him. The two said nothing along the short walk, and at once they were approaching the doors of the Gothic church whose doors were buttressed by two men who seemed to be talking to themselves and Blaise stared at their teeth until he saw that they were talking to one another. *It is good that they have one another in this lonesome world.* His mother said that to him after the divorce, in a room with big windows and light blue carpets and two cats who typically refused to interact chasing one another in a playful circles, circling in figure eights, the sign of infinity.

A huddle of old ladies in the back of the church started trading off parts of a litany, alongside them an Our Lady of Czestochowa. "The Black Madonna," Abdul said, and as his knees fell on the scarlet cushion set before the icon, Blaise saw tufts of dust cloud the space around the nave. Jesus's face was dark, and the Madonna's face was dark and scarred, but somehow the gilded, bejeweled crowns above their heads completed their faces, did not come off as counterpoints.

Abdul signaled for Blaise to kneel, but instead of cajoling him into praying, the man who had cut the chicken's head off only an hour earlier pointed up toward the top of a stained glass window, an image of Eden, emphasis on the angel's fiery sword, its flames flicking Adam and Eve away. At the very top one of the scarlet panels bordering the scene had been broken, the hole artless.

"I did it," Abdul said.

"You?" Blaise's eyes could not meet Abdul's, and so he stared up there at the hole with an almost devout intensity.

"This is the place that wants me to do the roof. *Not* fix the hole. Do the roof. Lay the tiles. I was outside one night. Doors to church locked and I wanted in. So bad. So bad. I wanted to scream and throw myself down on the floor. You ever laid down on marble floor? Very beautiful but shocks the shit outta you," he whispered now, just in case, but the ladies prayed their litanies as though no one else inhabited the church. "Shuts you up," he said. "Shuts you up. But I couldn't get in. Don't know what I did next. Went *crazy*. Threw the axe up through the window and came in through opening. Lay here. Long time. Lay here. No one noticed. No one except—. Picked it up. Put it in my pants like this, and, went home."

Blaise's eyes moved down from the hole, fixed on the angel guarding the gate of even—not even the angel but the angel's flaming sword, not even the flaming sword but the blade as sharp as the axe that had killed the chicken that would feed Abdul and his wife for a week until he would start to get under the table installments from the Church. Not even the blade but the orange aura of flame that guards the gates of Eden.

"Shuts you up," Blaise said.

"Out," said a voice, and the two men looked down the aisle to a voice that came from where darkness covered.

I. O. U.

ALEX'S ELBOW SNAPPED from the weight of his head, snapped like a merchant's scale under the heave of counterfeit weights, and he tensed as an unfamiliar hand snagged his collar and pulled him upright. He blinked wildly—blinked between flitting visions of last week's doctor's visit, the sweetly-spoken words *pulmonary embolism* and *heart*—then discreetly, as he started to smell and see where and with whom he was. He absorbed his surroundings quickly, as though to compensate for having clocked out for who knew how long. Alex's boss had reserved the cherry-stained round table situated at the center of the bar's *faux* suede backroom, directly beneath an archaic crystal chandelier that once hung from an Archbishop's mansion, that for many decades threw its fractured light in fits on invited dignitaries during the heady mid-century doctrinal debates, that was auctioned as the Church fought to pay sex-scandal fines without pulling too much from the pockets of the faithful.

Sounds started to make sense. A woman's disembodied voice, half-muffled and half-laugh, said *Stop it or I'll divorce you. I'm serious,* and, turning his head hungrily to locate its origin, Alex saw only the blue fluorescent of a flip phone in the outer dark lit only by low candles tucked into orbicular red holders. More familiar voices centered him. Co-workers said urgent things about impending projects, reports and data connected to past projects, and used words like *synergy* and *expedite* in copious quantities. His boss's lips were red from some coloring used in the raspberry liquor he liked best, but nobody wanted to say anything. He looked, his bar napkin smudged with spiced chicken grease, tucked into the hole of his loosened-tie, his cheeks large and happy and disconnected from the other parts of his face, something like an infant after a meal. This was the first time Alex had attended one of the newly-mandated "work meetings," which were held monthly at a downtown bar near the *Cosmoception* office but tucked into a largely abandoned neighborhood of mostly warehouses. The smile—which was more of a grimace— forced on Alex's faced began to cramp, when his best look of confidence threatened to collapse and leave him with nothing more than the lost look pining to be both seen and unseen at once.

His boss, Jay, talked to an audience of eight employees, even though his eyes looked no further than Elizabeth, the marketing consultant. Though he spoke as if to her alone, and though what he said seemed intimate enough that it could not have been intended for the whole crew, his words carried that weight that holds a crowd captive, seemingly by some combination of voluminous importance (a loud urgency of tone something like a knee-scraped child's), and that demeanor which makes one feel that when he does look at you he is in fact looking not at you but at an invisible mirror between you and him, and he is, in appreciating your presence, somehow appreciating himself, possibly unknowingly.

Jay was talking about his father, and how he had always wanted to really just sit down and talk with him, "but it just won't come. I wait and I wait but it just won't come. *I* put myself out there. *I* make the effort. 'Dad. Dad. *Do you know* me?' He'll turn. Sure. He'll say 'yes' or ask why the hell I would ask such a stupid question. But that's all I get, and he just sits there watching his shows. Staring off." At this Jay mimicked his father's vacated stare, not knowing that his imitation was hardly a stretch from the gaze he normally wore at the office when an underling arrived at the door, armed with questions a) b) c) or complaints about *x, y, z*. As he pandered on, his eyes—a sharp green that contrasted strikingly with his buzzed orange hair—were far more focused, were even wet around the edges, and reddened there like the rim of drink around his lips. The marketing assistant put her hand on his forearm, lightly, and then withdrew when Jay inhaled quickly, looked vigorously around the side room of the bar, as though the rest of the company had just snapped into existence.

The work meeting had started at *Cushion,* an upscale place whose margaritas started at fifteen dollars, but after he had passed around a printout on collaboration and teamwork, and after a few more minutes of decentralized discussions concerning all the employees not present, Jay had rounded up his faithful staff and insisted they move down to another bar, one by the old abandoned railroad tracks, named *Balzac's.* The one with the Archbishop's old chandelier. The fresh air and stretch would do the team good, he said. Studies had shown that workers don't do well when attentions spans are asked to stay steady for more than twenty minutes at once.

During this cab ride to what was for Alex an unknown dive, one of his co-workers, Derrick, informed the others, with a street-smart satisfaction, that *Balzac's* was a notorious cocaine bar, but that the cops normally left it alone. During the cab ride there, when Alex asked himself why he didn't merely open the door and roll out, asked himself what strange contract bound him to these co-workers who seemed so thrilled to be flinging across the city in the yellow bullet of the cab, on a Thursday evening, making silly faces to the "Middle Eastern" (Derrick used this adjective *humanely, openly*) music seeping through the bullet proof glass that separated the troupe from the driver, what had he done wrong, or right, that he had landed here? What professional sinews connected *Cosmoception,* which sold cutting-edge cosmetics, to a cocaine bar? And if none, then why not open the door, once the cab exited the interstate, and roll out of this one and into some other circuit of cabs and buses that could bring him back to his closet-sized apartment which, at this moment, would lose all of its claustrophobic characteristics as it let him leave this world, for a few hours, for the world of sleep?

Alex, like persons *a, b, c* to infinity, had graduated during the great recession. He spent endless hours filling out boilerplate forms on an increasingly blurrier screen. He spent months going through these motions, increasingly groaning as he filled in the blank spot next to Bachelors Degree:_____.
Humanities, he would write, most often, although sometimes *Liberal Arts* seemed more eloquent. No replies. Then rejection letters and emails mounted an offensive against his sense of self, and he began to feel weightless and light, detached from friends who held solid jobs, detached from the cashiers and the bag-ladies-and-gentlemen at the supermarket who had more dignity than he did, until he began to expand his market and make bids on any job under the sun, the sun which also rises, and, six months into the slog, he picked up his phone one day to hear the impossible words *like to interview you,* and he steadied himself against the refrigerator, which was filled with white bread and bologna-style deli meat, no more, and he said things he could not now remember, and said more things he could not now remember at three different interviews, after which he was handed an orientation folder that told him his purpose, which was to maximize grammatical and syntactical correctness on all of the company's internal communications: namely, mass emails from bosses to subordinates, the *Cosmoception* weekly newsletter, which established a sense of community among employees in disparate departments. And *yes, yes,* the voice on the other end of the phone had said, his degree in *Liberal Humanities* would more than qualify him, because *you had to do a lot of reading, no doubt. And you had to write a lot of papers. So you've got an eye for detail, and you've got more experience than you know. Look, I've been at this for a while, and what I'm about to say is no secret. Some would say you made bad choice in pursuing a humanities degree. And some would*

scold me for picking you up, to be frank, as you're just graduating from college. But in this case your 'experience' was part of your education.

But Alex was caught on *Liberal Humanities*, as the higher-up *face à face* must have mushed the two favored descriptions of what he'd devoted five years of his life to, and, in spite of that error, he had himself an interview, and soon he had himself a job. Family and friends rejoiced over the news: the hopeless case had managed at last. A week into the work he paused at least three times a day to shake his head over the fact that he had never garnered more respect in his life and yet had never done less work. After all, as a "supervisor" of a sub-department whose title he still had not memorized, but whose acronym spelled SASY, most days involved little more than four or five official *communiqué* and six or seven signatures on forms shoved under his paling, computer-lit face.

Through the thick, bullet-proof glass of *Balzac's* bar, Alex made out the face of a short man whose cheeks were so thin they dented in around his teeth, but whose head bulged out from the ears up, so that the whole was something like a pear. Hideous, on the one hand, but the effect was comic, for the eyes told Alex that this man, a *no man* in a nameless neighborhood of the city, either knew everything or imagined he did. That this man, covered in matching red sweatpants and jacket, scuffled—he limped, slightly, though he masked it—around the face of the earth unshaken by questions about himself or anyone else, and from boots to the glowing balding top of his head he carried a peculiar confidence that stole Alex's control over most of the muscles of his face.

The new customer planted himself alongside Alex at the roundtable, oblivious to the "meeting" which, via Jay's now voluminous confessions, had collapsed into swapped *father and son, mother and mother-in-law* stories. The man scanned the exposed portion of a newspaper Alex had not seen, but which was positioned in front of him as though he had been reading it. The new customer asked, "Anything in there about yesterday's murder?

The one with the man who was shot and killed at close range, one child under each arm. Just killed there waiting for the bus. Midday? Do you know?" he went on, his voice low and strained, like a wounded child's, until it snapped, lost its strain, but he went on rambling, as though audience was of no consequence.

"Did you know that the *criminal*, the one who did the killing, walked around the block, changed clothes—probably in some alleyway, or something—and returned to the spot to pick up the children. He held them there, each one squirming and shaking under his arm, until the police came. And then he told them everything that had happened. No one else had really *seen* it, although a couple of young women who worked at the diner down that way came out to tell that they heard the children crying for a few minutes. Well, they said, they had heard the children crying without knowing exactly what it was they had heard, and when they finally came out guess *who* was waiting there, holding the children."

"Anyhow," the man went on, running his large right hand over his head's sheen, "the man who did it told the diner ladies that the man who did the terrible thing had made off quickly, before our hero, who's soon enough standing there holding the children, could tackle him. He was still lifted on this doubled out amphetamine-marijuana high, see, this double man, this criminal-hero, or hero-criminal, see. He was still on this, this raise your mind above the sky if you know what I mean. And he came. Came to my hotel. Afterward. My brother. I'm staying in St. Louis, see? I's just in town for my brother, who said he's on the verge of something and needs me to come up for a while. Well, he's staying at this house where I'm not welcome, so I've been putting out fifty a week to get a room with a shared bathroom and sink and stove. You know, really homey kind of place," he went on, smiling for the first time, spittle falling and sparkling blue-red a bit in the orbiting bar lights.

"I've known him his whole life—" he broke off, and closed

his eyes spasmodically until little drips squeezed out. "Came to my house and confessed everything, the whole thing, hugging me the whole time like I was his closest friend—which, being his brother and that, sure, I guess, but look out now for Cain and Abel. Cause he had a jackknife to me the whole time. Shit. The thing about his confession was. Was," Alex watched the man's mouth the whole time he talked, in a low tone, the opening of his mouth aimed just right so that Alex and Alex alone could hear what he said. Burning up a bit, sweat soaking the V-neck of his undershirt, Alex looked quickly out of the bullet-proof glass whenever eye contact was close at hand.

"Well, he confessed it. He told me in great detail of the man's eyelashes, which, he said, he counted, and found some fifty of them. He told me how terrible it all became, because even though his pulse was pushing blood on and on he stared and stared out of the corner of his eye at the neon red letters of the digital clock down the street, the one above the fluorescent *LOTTERY* sign, and it did not change. Did not change. But there was no *woe is me,* no I'm sorry or shame. It was. He was!" he whispered now, but with spittle excitedly spraying Alex.

"Was not sorry at all. Told me directly. Was not sorry at all. 'Why'd you do it?' I asked him, the knife still hovering around my liver, poking my skin every, maybe, few seconds. 'Motive?' he said back, getting mad. 'Everybody wants a motive, so they can make their damn peace with it or something. Have it figured out and go to sleep a little easier. But I,' he finished, and I could feel his breath, 'I *needed* to do it. It's been following me around for my whole life now. Death. Had to see it happen. And I figured, well, this man's continued his line, had his babies, you understand? And so it was easier, somehow. Because—. The shot came. And there it was, so quick. So quick. All gone man. And there it was. And, man, all my suspicions were right. Something's wrong with us if the only stakes we got are life or death. Because they's nothing, you see. Some kind of—illusion.' And he went on about medicine, and how it was the people who supposed to save a life who are the ones who kill people. Cleanly, though, cleanly. Negligence—quietly, the kind of thing where X number of accidental deaths caused by doctor negligence shows its monstrous face in no other way than higher insurance rates. I remember—when he said, *monstrous*. And he wasn't having it. He was going to make the world messy, he said. He was going to make good people shake a little at the dinner table, if they even dared to read the stories about him. And they would, he said. *Why* he still hadn't figured, but knew he was on to something. And then he said, 'Listen, I'm gonna be real with you, straightforward, bro. You're not by any count safe.' But I. Need someplace to stay tonight. And I knew when I went in here, I knew even looking in that fat window o'er there that you the one, the one I got to ask. You got a place. And you not so jaded like them other twenty folks I been asking tonight. Now, can I get an amen? Am I right? You got *humanities.*"

At *humanities* Alex perked up, as though he were in a new interview now, as though some consequential decision maker from the upper echelons of government had beckoned him for an interview, laid before him some dilemma and, in spite of his superior knowledge of statecraft, admitted his befuddlement: "But you, with your degree in the humanities. Young man you have to know what to do." Then the perk fizzed out, like the stomach tablet the man next to him dropped into the icy water glass, not caring whose water it was originally, just draining the whole thing heartily, licking the stippled flecks of medicine from his teeth at the end, awaiting some sign of Alex's *humanities.*

"Well," Alex said, at last, "I guess I got some *humanities.* I did get my degree in it."

"What you mean?" the man asked, shaking the ice around the glass like dice for a game of craps. "A degree in *humanities*? I'm talking 'bout your *spirit.* I can see—between you and me— that yours is real. Is lit up like."

"You mean my mind," Alex answered, and, retreating into a discourse he half-thinkingly hoped would push the man away, he said, "*Espirit.* In French *Espirit, spirit,* means *mind.* If that's what you mean, you got something. But I have no *spirit.* I'm flesh, man, from my feet to my brain. Even my *spirit* is flesh."

The man pushed away from the table edge a bit, and swiveled back and forth in the somewhat ratty blue chair, studying Alex. "Man, maybe I was wrong." Then, looking down for a time, shutting his eyes as if in prayer, he said, "You fucked up, man? You driving home?"

"Look, I got some cash I can give you. Get a hotel or whatever." Alex had trouble hearing his own voice over the crowd, whose voice strove collectively toward some voluminous summit that would be audible over the cymbals and distorted guitar that sprang from the speakers like some primordial urge.

"Man, forget it," the man said. "Forget it, man," and, bouncing off the chair, he stood up and walked away, shaking his head as he went through the welcome door and out of sight.

Alex checked on his co-workers, most of whom slurred words now, slipped loosely into one another's space, and as Jay and Elizabeth rose to leave together, the former shouting "Meeting adjourned" in self-mockery, others followed. At once Alex gasped. Could not find his breath. Could not follow them into their cabs, could not watch them grope one another cautiously—or, rather, could see himself letting that be done to him and doing it to some blurry soul himself—and yet could not remain at the table alone, marked as an outsider in this notorious bar.

He brushed past a woman whose *Cosmoception* desk was three doors down, consented to her uncensored eyes and then, his hand against the door, let the rush of outside air shake him loose. He felt the pain in his knees, the one his doctor said would get worse so long as he sat at a desk all day without exercise breaks, without at the very least some toe-touches every half an hour, and felt it pierce and then fade away as he ran after the man, the man whose bald head glowed down the block, glowed and then went out as he moved between streetlights.

"Wait!" he hailed, as though desperate for a cab, as though calling after the last cab of the evening, the only ride that could get him out of this godforsaken place. He hurried now, hurling his body toward the man as though from the top of a building, as though testing *humanity*, checking whether anything in him would intervene to protect his act of compassion, whether he could stave off self-interest and the urge for survival long enough to help someone who was wrung around the neck with ropes he knew he himself had never and would never know. No. Nearing the man, who had stopped and was sitting, elbows on knees, on the steps at the base of someone's porch, Alex admitted—for a fragment of an instant—that he *was* testing something else. For, footage of his co-workers collapsing onto one another reeling through his head, he couldn't conjure up hope in sheer *humanity* any longer.

"Look," he said, emptying his right pocket of cash, his left hand touching his back butt pocket to be sure that fifty still remained there. This, he told himself, was the *least* he could do. This was nothing, now that the *Cosmoception* job was dropping disposable income into his account every two weeks—a phenomenon he'd never known and one that didn't thrill him as much as he thought it might, now that he could buy all the albums and all the lunches-out he'd like. "Here," he held it out. "I don't know what you want, man. But take it. Take it." Of course he had loans, some $88,345, due in monthly installments of $585, but *Cosmoception* paid well, coated him in a powdery comfort that kept fiscally-motivated palpitations at bay.

The furrows of the man's forehead, the base of the upside-down pear, filled out. He held out his left hand, moved it past the cash and beckoned Alex's left hand forward. It obeyed. "I'm David," the man said. "Man, you talking to me like I's robbing you or some shit. 'Take it, take it!' I ain't doing that, man. I just need some *body*. I'll tell you," he went on, signaling so that Alex would sit next to him on the crumbled concrete step, on the sidewalk chalk pictures scrawled there by some child: fat cats and numbers, a great big fish. "Between you and me. I'm *scared. I'm* scared. Maybe that's what's getting you all mussed up. Contagious or what. I don't need money but a safe place. I want money I can..." He paused. "Look, I'll be real. *I* know how to get it. Money. Man. But I don't know if I'm live the night to get it or anything else if I don't find—some *place.*"

Alex considered the crow-dark sky. The skyscraper lights that loomed, some miles away, like man-made stars, constellations conjured with full randomness from the offices of workaholics. He considered his life, how he'd landed the job at last and still felt, or felt even more, his own meaninglessness. How inconsequential his own absence from this city would be. How only an encephalitic ego could claim otherwise. And so what if David did him in. Killed him off. Worst case scenario. What we always tell ourselves we do for the world how much of it can't stand up to the simplest questions and maybe my little contribution to humanity could be shortening my own little life so that somebody else can take my job can make my money and know better what to do with it I don't know feed some children or pay for some college or build some water well in some Sahara. Shit.

ALEX'S studio apartment was slim by any standard. A woman he'd had over once told him it was smaller than the mud hut she'd lived in in the Nigerian bush. A body could lay flat across the floor in one of two places: on the bed, which swung down from a hinge on the wall, and in the bathtub, which hadn't been cleaned well for months. When he first moved in even he was sickened by the filth, and he went to work scrubbing at the blackened mold and the green stains with bleach until his head lightened and he floated like a balloon to bed. And slept, as soundly as David did now, in the bathtub, where the guest insisted he should sleep, deserving no more than that. *Than what?* Alex now asked himself. Than a hard ceramic pillow, a faucet for a footrest, a stinky jacket for a blanket.

It could have been hours that he spent there, sitting awake, comforted by his own shivers because they served as insurance against any chance of drifting off into sleep, his chattering eyes swiveling between David's head, which barely peeked above the bathtub rim, and the toilet across from him.

And then he shook the man. The plan came at once. He couldn't take it anymore, this trying to trust *humanity,* his own or anyone else's. He would speak excitedly of a nearby diner's breakfast special, present it as part of his daily ritual. He would buy the breakfast David had never eaten. And, getting up to use the bathroom, he would shoot out the door and head to *Cosmoception.* But the shaken man did not move. His brown face, gray from light that filtered through the frosted bathroom window, feigned no sleep, and neither did it speak of irritation at the jolt. It simply did nothing.

Alex bent over him. Felt his forehead for—what, a fever? The greasy skin felt freezing through and through, though Alex could not definitively attribute it to David, as his own hands had lost feeling long ago, blood cut from them as they rested under him, as he kept his trustless vigil. Frantic, Alex rubbed his own hands against his own knees, not knowing what he was doing. Darting over to the faucet. Turning hard. Turning it on. The hot water.

"Agk man! What kinda shit?" David said, and, forging little open slits in his eyes, checking things over in the most cursory fashion, he fell back asleep. But only fully for a moment, before his hands started moving, with irritation and rapidity, over the buttons of his shirt, the elastic waistline of his red sweatpants, until he'd stripped himself thoroughly and lay with absolute nakedness without shame before Alex, who scurried to the cabinet, snatched a few satchels of powder soap samplers the marketing man from *Cosmoception* had given him, and dumped them all—*Lavender, Claret, Lime-Coconut*—into the bath, which he could not believe was not burning the man, as the steam whispered profusely over everything until surreality was supreme.

Seconds later the mist disappeared, and Alex stared at David's body, buried to the stomach by assorted soap bubbles. Alex could not unfix his gaze from what first looked like a badly done scarlet tattoo, almost three-dimensional on the skin above his heart, *in fact* three dimensional on the skin above his heart: the sketch looked something like that wound of God he'd seen in dimly lit, green-carpeted grade school halls.

"My brother," David said. "Don't know if I told you. My brother—he done some time as a tattoo artist. He did this. Said he was gonna gimme that free tat he been talking about for years. But shit it felt too painful to be—and then he did *this* to me. Cut around the tat I'd had done when I was sixteen. A heart. A girl. You know how I mean, man. To let me know he's serious. Cut it in me yesterd—." He swallowed the last word, a choke, which turned into a laugh. "Tell you what. Now this embarrassing me. Can you. Can you wipe this clean? Take a piece of toilet paper, maybe. Just wipe off the blood. I'm clean man, I'm. Can you just wipe it? I don't know. Some reason it scares the shit outta me every time I think about it. God knows I can hardly look at it. Touch it."

Already Alex had unrolled a sheet of toilet paper, a brittle brand a bit tough to the touch, and, now opening the medicine cabinet and soaking it with some five-year-old antiseptic he hoped held potency, he knelt beside the bathtub and leaned in toward David and started to touch a corner of the folded-over square to the edge of this sacred heart, the thick lines that separate shards of stained glass, cut deep into his skin. His hand felt stilted and he steeled himself, squinting to see the wound with full clarity, drawing strength from the long forgotten but familiar scene of one of the sisters, the only full nun still teaching at the private school his parents sent him to strictly for its fine academic standing, though they considered Jesus an overall good influence: Health class, the same lime green carpet that covered the entire school, the same cobalt blue chalkboard, thick chunks of chalk overflowing in the gutter below. Pails even lower, pails he'd need to fill after school, fill with warm sudsy water. David covered in soap. David's heart. David's heart the nun in front of the class, another teacher wheeling in a mannequin on a stretcher and the nun now with her own pail of sterile water, some pungent substance potent in the pail. Wringing out a sponge and wiping red marker-made lines signifying wounds on the plastic person, wiping straight from his right shoulder down and diagonal toward his left side, smiling without trying with no sappiness at all. Alex knowing then when he grew up he would be a doctor or a nurse. The nun said this is the sort of thing you could do with your life: tend to Christ. He saw the glint in her eyes, the brown eyes that matched the brown habit that hid most of her from the world, most but her hands he could see them all, tending so gently to the sick mannequin, and him, and now recalling her motions and making them his, cleansing the carved heart that, blood sopped up now, looked more than ever like the sacred heart of the hallways, and David's eyes too like long hallways leading he knew not where, drops of wet gathering there that were not the water no they came from inside him and neither knew what to say but David said, "I owe you one," laughing a wet-eyed laugh, "I owe you one bro," as Alex, jolted by what by the thought of debt, of *I owe you,* said "Shit, I got to get to work. I'm late" and he stepped back, the toilet paper pink and red, dropped it into the trash.

"Stay here," he said, reaching his finger behind him until it touched a tie, swinging it around his neck in some semblance of a knot. Smelling himself then, smelling the traces of the night's trustless vigil, no time to take a shower, and Jay was not one to notice wardrobe repetition.

He dropped a few things into a safe his father had bought him once, birth certificate and some old pictures and books—is that all he really had that he found worth protecting against theft?—and then dousing himself with the cheap cologne his father bought him for his birthday as he walked down the hall. As the elevator opened and the metallic rectangle swallowed him and carried him closer to his career of *choice*. "*Of choice*," he scoffed, and, descending in solitude as his stomach ascended, he steadied himself against the shimmering gray side. *What choice did I have? What chose me?* The two questions wrecked against one another as two mistimed trains. *What choice did I have what chose me* what with the market? To market to market this jiggidy jig, but home again home again against the grain. To ask what do I want to *be* when I grow up. Like a child again. *What choice did I have who chose me* he asked, one last time, and this time the loop of the question mark snagged his head like a shepherd's staff and reeled him back toward David, the man in his bath.

Just before he pressed a button that would have sent him back home, the elevator door split open and three men, one of whom he recognized from some *Cosmoception* connection, rushed in. He tried to hide from the man's eyes, but they waited patiently, their thick eyebrows raising and lowering patiently until Alex felt he had no choice. And he went to work, "networking," listening to chatter about other *networking*, and *synergy*, and *expedite* as the metallic rectangle reached the first floor. The others exited, but as he moved toward the now-closing doors he found he was too late, stuck inside in spite of hands beating haphazardly against all buttons. And then he saw his sallow face reflected against the dull bronze elevator walls that surrounded him he breathed, and breathed again, and it was impossible, yes it was, that the palpitation was gone. *I owe you*, he said, thinking of the way that tattooed heart seemed to pump outward until it filled the entire cosmos, beating through the blood of how many.

Everything Must Go

MR. COLE FEDD, founder of Fatt Fedd's Ice Cream, found innocent in a case that brought him the stardom of nearly international scandal, literally did not know the meaning of the word *vacation*. His skin, except for the pockets of saggy flesh which guarded his eyes, was unfailingly tan, and his dyed blonde hair looked, one journalist noted, "like the standard Cancun wig for old men just vain enough to primp their looks, but just artless enough to show the seams of a life of quietly riotous desperation." This, though, was due only to compressed trips to the tanning booth and barber: the very thought of leisure gave Mr. Fedd a kind of *delirium tremens*. If our hero had known the meaning of the word *vacation* it would have been anything but easy for him to call up his secretary, complain briefly but without passivity about the hallmarks of a hangover in her already ornery tone, and say, "Listen. I'm going on vacation," and her suddenly steady and empathic rebound, "Well, yes, well God you need one if anyone does. Can I tell inquirers where?" to his "The middle of nowhere."

Looking back years later, after a rigorous reeducation that would have made President Machel's reeducation camps in Mozambique in the (same) eighties (in which a former Hollywood actor was President of the United States) look rational, he would comprehend, memorize, accept, and believe in many things that he did not now, one of these things being the somewhat complex phrase, "I'm going on *to be empty*," as well as some of the reasons that *she*, that is *She*, his first love now long lost, went to Mozambique after reading a waiting room copy of the

New Yorker, a featured report on the post-communist state of that country. He said, "Don't get all political on me" after, in Her second sentence She started in with the word *injustice.* He had never heard of Mozambique when She said it, and had placed it at first in the Middle East. He felt further disorientation when, after their tense conversation, he had dug out a world map from a musty basement box and found Mozambique bordering the southeastern coast of Africa. And she left that same night, a nocturnal flight with four layovers. He took her to the airport like a cabdriver, she in the backseat, him bleating out the occasional small talk.

"Sure is dark. That neon really gets to the eyes when it's the only thing that's glowing."

"…"

"Sure are a lot of layovers."

She made some comment about saving money so that she would have more for the people there, the Mozambicans. Some bullocks that was to make her majestic before him, that did in fact make her majestic so that the scarlet leather interior was at once a sacramental royal. In reply, he indulged in elaborations regarding a business trip he once took to India, a first class flight on which he sampled mango ice cream almost twice an hour and ordered a massage from a young hostess three times, each followed by a hot facial towel in case, he said, in a joke that came out like a sour, sickening belch, the lipstick stuck. Things sped up then, as the car swung right toward the airport exit. She said she would mail him back her airplane peanuts, for when his business started shaking. Because it would, she said. It would. It was just a matter of time, she said, and he would be hungry. And he would see how starving his artifice had made him. She said these things with a softness in her voice, the chimeric softness of a run-of-the-mold grandmother and doctor blended into one, a voice at once professionally concerned and arthritic enough that anything it said could be received without rash resentment. She used that word, too: *artifice.*

But if her words tickled his vanity he soon enough blew them off like white dandelion wisps, turning his head as the seedlings embedded themselves elsewhere, rebounding off the indifferent world that revolved, that revolutionized around him.

And then she wrote him on the bloody public medium of the post card and said, *I am here, on the continent that claims the origins of humankind. I am working on clean water. The view from here is glory, I guess. Painful glory, and down to earth is anything but. You can't be. That is, everything is elevated, in my mind. This is not a cry for help, or to make you come after me like the hero you never said you were, never saw you did but clung to being. I am working on empty, but I am fine. I thought of you because last week, on a day without water to distribute we came across some ice cream and gave that away instead. It was all fun and games, all at once. I am officially vacating, I suppose. Vacation. From the Latin* vacare, *meaning, "to be empty."*

I scream. You scream. We all scream. Ice cream.

THAT was the thing that had turned their passing along a crowded sidewalk into a night of stealing glances across the round emerald table of a smoky Irish pub.

"*Pulcher,*" he had said, startled by his own boldness, caught by the nets of lashes around her.

"*Advocate nostrae—illa pulchrae est,*" she responded, startling him again as she reached down her blouse, her hand between her breasts while they moved out of the stream of people. Under the soft light of a chocolate shop she pulled out, hung at the end of a silver chain, a medal of the Mother of God, her head crowned with stars, her hands stretched out in both abandonment and supplication at once. He watched her watching the medal, startled a third time as she sung out, "*O-o-o-o-O dulcis, Virgo Maria,*" the sweet melody literally lifting him up on to his tiptoes, so that when she finished he looked down awkwardly, found his footing awkwardly, embarrassed and enthralled by his departure from the down-to-earth demeanor by which he defined himself.

Her frequent use of Latin was so much a part of her that it served as one of those incongruous traits that did not fit but made her somehow more strange, more exotic. The blood-red strands that sprouted without dye amidst her dandelion-yellow hair. The tattoo of prisoner 0345668's number, someone whom, before she returned to the Catholic faith of her youth, she had written to through Amnesty International, then dated when his death row sentence was cut short. Cropping up again and again: the compulsive and somewhat solemn use of Latin. Corollary questions hounded him. A habit? An escape from the mess of the modern world? Was their bond based on common renunciations, selective cynicism, even if they had never overtly spoken so? She had received some sort of parochial education. She sucked in her top lip until it turned dark whenever he asked about Her past, or when he asked anything in a manner that displayed too much curiosity and not enough trust. *Fides,* She said, not giving him a further reason. He told her that he was a searcher, but after he did so he mocked himself internally, disgusted by the lethargic pace of his search. "I'm searching for *You,*" he shouted into the darkness, back upon his bed, body cocooned under a brown wool blanket. And then he spat at the thought of that *Virgo Maria* who guarded the breasts and the body that, he knew, would bring the end of his search. The familiar image of repressed nuns strapped into tight-necked habits, releasing their rage through rulers and Latin grammar lessons: *ablative plural, ablative plural, again and again.* On saints' feast days they would lick cones filled with vanilla bean, homemade treats applying the mother superior's ancient recipe. The next day it would be ruler and Latin all over again. Carnival to famine to keep them hungry. Not far from some of the principles he had learned during his MBA night classes.

HE tore the postcard out of his home office later. After he, his own boss, called in to work. He tore it off the cork board and two tacks fell, bounced, and disappeared somewhere atop the scrupulously polished floorboards. He wanted to bring the postcard with, on his vacation, because it had a picture of the sunset as can be seen only from the coast of Mozambique, and he was going north, into a coastless cold world whose sun gave light but not heat. Where the whole earth became a veritable snow cone. Mr. Fedd saw—fleeting vision as he shut his eyes—firefighters dropping buckets of Fatt Fedd's ice cream syrup upon the vanilla earth. *Making the world just a little bit sweeter, a little bit lighter,* went the slogan, signaling the low-calorie mission of the company.

After turning the sun in slow spirals on his knee, he turned the postcard over and read the back over and over as the car continued obediently toward *vacation* and he reached into his travel bag to make sure he had packed enough mouthwash. Malcolm, bright eyes big in the rear view mirror, steadied the vehicle with even greater skill when he saw his boss fidgeting with an artifact of apparent import. In this way Mr. Fedd read the whole letter flawlessly as the car traversed a road of uneven gravel and what could have been groaning peaks and valleys. The sedan speakers played soft, instrumental sounds made by a chorus of recorded flutes. She had given him that, too. *What an idiot I was*, he breathed out, a bass note covering over his confession, and as the song climbed the scale he stared down that rectangle of himself that fit the rear view, trying to find traces of the fool who took the gifts she gave him as a parent takes the trivial things his children present as treasures. Mr. Fedd asked Malcolm to please let the thirty minutes of music play circularly, repeatedly, until they reached the heart of the middle of nowhere.

AND then he was, he *was*, caught up in a flitting consciousness of his own being, horrified by the unknowing insects that crawled across an orb web. An ample spider ruled the ceiling corner from the upper echelons of the taut radials of spider silk, laissez-fare written all over its threadbare designs, as if its kingdom had come and gone and there was little to work for anymore. Mr. Fedd's slunk positioning made three folds appear around his neck, and after cleansing them of sweat rivulets with straight and uninterrupted flicks he chortled his nostrils clear and reached for his breast pocket as if of his nakedness he was entirely unawares. An abundance of ants or gnats or some other tribe of insects identifiable to men with greater vision than those there present paraded beneath the cobweb, the wispy cobweb strung out around the light and splintering the light and fixing thin shadows onto the cherished refuge, the cherry wood sauna set some six miles into the pine wood haven Mr. Fedd referred to as "my mistress," although he was not married and had never been and generally—except in the case of Her—avoided things common to love.

Mr. Fedd's Senior Advisor, naked but for a towel, who had met him in this remote nowhere of the earth, sat across from his superior and squinted at the empty web until a run of wrinkles dominated his still childlike face. "Anyways, it's always, a, it's always a question of costs expended versus prospective gains, isn't it, right?" he asked with a sigh that left a serious desire in the room, in both men. The Senior Advisor eyed the spider with resentment, dipping his dried elbow into a tin of balm and rubbing it in hard, massaging it up his entire arm which changed from pasty white to near-bronze as he did so.

After a few moments sewed themselves into a pall of silence, the Senior Advisor firmed up the nerve to speak again in the same manner that he would firm himself in rising elevators before meeting with prospective distributors. His boss's inexplicable sleepiness wearied him and made it hard for him to recall just how long they had been in heat, which made it impossible to say with certainty whether they had overstayed the recommended forty-five minute limit for saunas set at ninety degrees. Thin wisps of smoke emerged from the rocks set above the heater in the sauna's corner. Above the thin wisps of smoke the spider hung above its prey. The Senior Advisor casually leaned over, threw his balm tin at the empty web, hung his head between his ankles and said, "Goddamn footies don't stop you from slipping," nodding at the blue foot guards applied from a dispenser at the door. Mr. Fedd did not follow the tin toward its target, nor did he reply. Nor did he budge when the clang came and sent out the initial sound in circling echoes. He began to breathe in deep heaves, rhythmic and intentional. Softer, but still aloud the Senior Advisor gave his boss an earnest head shake, let his eyes rest on the man's off-yellow hair, and added, "If people only knew that this world doesn't go round without quite a few of us getting gray or bald early. Sure enough would have no hair left myself if it wasn't for the surgery. I'd, I don't think you could know how much it means to me that the company footed the bill." He seemed to realize at that moment that he was not bald anymore, that under that toupee Mr. Fedd was, and that what he said was impolite at best, imbecilic at worst—either way a tally against him to be conjured at some distant review. He caught, out of the corner of his eye, the elaborate web still sparkling in the sauna mist. "Slipped," he said, then straightened his back and leveled some of his belly folds, helping one of them over the towel rim.

"Vacation, please, vacation please. Vacation *por favor*," Mr. Fedd said, like the judges in the movies and daytime television specials popular toward the winter of his youth, those who said, "Order in the court, order in the court, *order in the court*." As soon as he said this he sputtered his lips, horse-like. The judge who decided his case was decidedly more pedestrian, and more surprising than the verdict of innocence was the wonder that the man had passed his law school exams. At least that's what Mr. Fedd had said, running his hand through his dyed blonde toupee, to his Senior Advisor, who sometimes felt like a childhood friend tolerated out of loyalty, sometimes like a tour guide, protecting him from the underbellies and underscoring the brighter sides of the company and of reality.

Then Mr. Fedd's shoulders went back and it seemed he was piercing the walls and staring down some noble aim—a pose worthy of a marble bust in some bygone age of great men, of heroes and statesman and public servants. The Senior Advisor had seen a room of such busts once when he took Mr. Fedd's mother to the Art Museum when the boss was called to an unexpected board meeting. And he had said to Fedd's mother: "Your son is at home in this room, ma'am," and she straightened her mauve triangular collar along the length of her shoulder, set her head back a bit and said, "Little Cole. I never thought he would have made a good king, but, yes, yes this place—regal. He would be, is what I mean."

Mr. Fedd snapped his Senior Advisor out of the museum, out of all musings. "Now I could be wrong. Seems possible, especially with the messes driving me out of my mind lately. And you're in charge of my itinerary. But this little getaway isn't supposed to be a gripe session, or a eulogy, or anything familiar at all. Nothing at all is supposed to be familiar here, is it? let's… um, well," he wiped a small pocket of sweat from the crevice opposite his elbow and it hit the ground heavily, "live."

From the corner came the sauna's entire source of light, so looking there was something like looking into the sun. The Senior Advisor looked there fiercely as soon as Fedd's voice raised, and it stayed there afterward. Around the halogen the cherry wood looked especially fine, and the skill of the woodworker and stainer stood most naked and most lovely. The late wind let out a lame yelp, a hound too old to do much besides whine for death like a younger dog would for a mate.

Mr. Fedd heaved a few breaths out and said, "It's a damn shame I got no one to share this place with," and pressed a finger near each ear to ward off all objections. He proceeded to stare in the direction of the spider web, not actually seeing anything but a blurry orb. He did not sit up indignant, as he would have were he not on vacation. He did not clamor for the Senior Advisor to get up and get Malcolm out of the warm car and fire up the soldering gun and fill the godforsaken holes that yawn so wide it's no wonder there's a colony of disgusting insects in here. Instead he repeated something She had once said, spoke it with the same verve and intensity she had.

"Thrownness. We are *thrown* into the world, you know this? By the time we are here, I mean in awake in a way that that spider, with all of its instinctual cunning, will never be, we are already *thrown*. How can you *not* see *vacare* at the heart of it all? You, with your spreadsheets and figures—what if underneath it all there's nothing? Your rubrics and measurements wish to know nothing of this nothing. *Nothing.*"

The Senior Advisor was straight-backed and eyes shut. He kept his lips together tight, awaiting an order like an infantryman or fast food employee on the breakfast shift, an employee you have seen and can see now and will continue to see, gaze dulled by that odd cosmos comprised of grease, grill, and neon lights.

When he peeked he saw that Mr. Fedd's eyes were as wide as his mind and his mind seemed to project upon the sauna wood in strings of thoughts so lucid, so light, that they blotted out the shadowy web. But when he closed his eyes, Mr. Fedd became esoteric and his glazed face painted the room with a harsh opacity. Indeed, Mr. Fedd had not, even in the throes of wasted youthful nights, given credence to the thoughts that dove like gulls in the wake of that beautiful string of philosophical crumbs she had left him with. He started to write, as if in apology: *Feels stupid, really. Giving this a shot. Not going to go in for a therapist. Anything but that. If this works I'll be damned but the only woman I ever loved kept one and she swore by it, and by the way she was the only woman I ever talked to who I can say with utmost confidence actually listened to me. Listened. Listen. God, why have I spent myself searching for one after another after another sets of ears—that's it—ears alone!* And here he broke off, dizzied as he watched a reel of all the interviews of underlings he had ever conducted, all of these interviewees represented here with huge ears, some so large that between them he could hardly make out the faces. *I don't know the last time I listened to a single son of—*.

He wrote this on a candy wrapper spread out across the first page of a daily pocket journal, which he had brought within in spite of the damage that would necessarily result. He had the thing propped open on the edge of his thigh, its pale leathery cover folded upright as though it was an outgrowth or a benign abscess. A pen with a nostalgic nose let out thoughts like so many fireflies feigning the luminosity of neon lights. He could throw away the wrapper if this didn't work. If it did, maybe he would dare write in the thing itself. Having options was especially helpful. Like picking out shades of dye for the ice cream before the product assumed a veritable permanence out in the world, out on the market. When he wrote he pressed the pen hard, through the wrapper and into the notebook, as though quickly engraving obscenities into a school desk, and the golden nib reflected sparks of light just as violently toward the disbelieving gaze of his Senior Advisor.

Mr. Fedd remembered when he and his brothers had discovered their father's journal—blue leather cover bleached by years of sun—after his death. At the top of each page a date, and nearly none of the pages full. List after list of things done that day. A form that kept the *thrownness* at bay:

Fixed the garage door. Lunch with Aunt Viola. She's getting treatment for bad circulation

Cole's second birthday. Made him pancakes but told him either sugar or honey but not both.

Cole drew a strange comfort from his father's form, and picked up where the old man had left off:

Fix the insect problem here. Fix Malcolm a cup of hot chocolate when he drops us at the lodge. Where did I put that book on servant leadership? Scratch that. Throw the damn thing out. As though I'm a horse that needs bridle and bit. Tips from other men half as successful. Senior Advisor needs new suit. Tell him gently. The emperor has no clothes. *Breakfast with Uncle Al before departure—does he think less of me now that.../Remember, no more coffee meetings with Paulo, not alone. He gets too familiar./ American Ginseng instead of Coffee. Less Jitters./Does mom still have my childhood devotional? Do I own a book of prayers?/Bring Jim M with if meetings with Paulo are unavoidable/ $Deposit 4,457/Read article on Chinese Chewing Gum (a change in line of work instead of selling out and early retirement)? On the seventh day God rested.*

He wrote stolidly, dappling his own thoughts with a rare thought here and there. And yet was it this thought that set him loose, lifted the feeling that a mousetrap copper strip was pressed against his neck, keeping him quieter than a... Then, a snap—his Senior Advisor cracking his neck, and something else internal. He sneered at the entire game of words before him. The way the only woman he had ever loved seemed to write so consciously, as though—he had scathingly suspected—everything jotted was only done so in the case that fame find her someday and some troop of urban archaeologists show up at her Manhattan studio apartment and search the place for any old scrap, any old *revelation.*

It was good that we broke things off. Mr. Fedd almost said, then, "You ever loved anybody?" aloud. Somehow he was sure that the Senior Advisor was in fact married. Not that love and marriage necessarily—*shit.* His own thoughts were starting to sharpen in a way that he did not like. He needed the Senior Advisor, and twisted his feet around one another, seeing that he had uttered irretrievable and upsetting words. He needed him.

"Sweat," said the Senior Advisor as he wiped his eye, although they both knew it was a tear. "It's lonelier, sometimes, when you're with somebody else who's supposed to take *that* away if nothing else."

"The subject of one thousand popular songs," said Mr. Fedd, failing again to curb his tongue, which the years had sharpened into an icepick.

"Still I'm circling around those same promises I made on our wedding day," said the Senior Advisor. "There is no beginning or end. The circle. The ring," he said, and the eyes of each went to the Senior Advisor's ring, which soaked up the halogen and shot it back out with greater brilliance and beauty.

With sudden vigor, Mr. Fedd found his pen forming an inky, bleeding circle as he remembered the hastily-constructed outdoor ice skating rink beyond the increasingly claustrophobic sauna. The ice-rink kit he had spontaneously ordered a day or two ago. The hour he spent earlier, scuffing the frozen surface made by the all-purpose Malcolm (*technically my valet*) and cutting a rotund figure eight repeatedly without giving a damn as to whether his well-combed hair maintained its casually gelled waves; the checkered scarf given him by his mother from that last pinpoint of memory burning through her dementia—black and blue squares; this invigorating chill followed an unexpected cup of hot white chocolate waiting in the sedan cup holder and referenced nonchalantly by valet, as though it had simply appeared. And then. And then, on Malcolm's recommendation, Fedd was driven some goodly miles into the snowed out woods, to the sauna which he had never visited alone—the one where he had, at a very low tide in life, taken *Her*. After they had broken things off. A weekend's worth of both trying to figure out how to touch one another in spite of the surety that this was the end. And then, like two dissatisfied moviegoers, they left one another after the matinée of their predictable Sunday brunch break up.

And I think it was Malcolm who found me in the sauna and who said it isn't right for a man to be alone. Malcolm, when have you ever been anything but alone? Maybe that's how you know?

Just before he had leaped from the sedan, Mr. Fedd had snapped the door shut and asked Malcolm with tightly pressed lips to please return in twenty minutes to pick up the Senior Advisor.

"It isn't right to be alone. Who said that?" he asked.

"God," Malcolm had said, and Mr. Fedd searched his eyes for a wink but found none.

"Well, God might be right but I—need to figure something out that I have a feeling I can only figure out if I'm alone."

"Sir?" Malcolm had said. In spite of the innocent verdict, and in spite of Fatt Fedd's rebounding and even rocketing success, She was right about that *thrownness* and the things it did to you. "Sir I don't recommend your being alone out here *now*," Malcolm said.

He caught himself before he asked, "What was his name again?" It was unlike him to be so estranged and he said this aloud as he clicked off the padlock and pried open the door. He was accustomed to using an employee's name with great frequency and found value in exclaiming his indebtedness to those who did well by him: should he do some shopping for himself, even the grocer's name was learned and used at least three times before the transaction ended. He was not fond of the theatrics of distance. He was at base a Midwestern boy, raised for much of his youth on a military base. Raised on white bread, ketchup spaghetti, and canned wax beans. Potatoes. Never far the instructional reminiscences of parents: "During the thirties we made salads out of the tree leaves," and his father's prayerfully-repeated: "Sending you to school is for me just as good as sending myself." He did not even mind the probability, the pressure that he was for his father a chance at fulfilling vacated, failed paths. It was something to live for. It was a good life, his. Was. It. Was. It. Mr. Fedd inked a page break and tore part of the page in the process. Sideways he wrote: *It is taking Malcolm far too long. It is taking Malcolm far too long.*

Above each word he placed eighth notes at varying heights. As though he knew how to play let alone read music. Was he getting prayerful? He flicked his ear and felt the spray that followed. He should be going. He should be getting on with his life. This was not working out, this vacation. Or it was working too well. It was more of an evasion than anything.

A cooked and civilized chicken, he wrote, and sketched a pathetic poultry whose head hung from its rubbery neck. The Senior Advisor knew the look that he now received, a look that often came when a deal was going badly, and he nodded and reached for their hooked jumpsuits.

Mr. Fedd's last words, written perfectly across the blue guiding crosslines, rang with bold claims about human existence: *I realize this is boring but this is the stuff of life and if I cannot get through the dullness I might as well call it a day* followed by *maybe I should write an autobiography? How many kids work for some jerk just because they fear the unknown, they don't know the 'How To's' of being your own boss.* And then, at the very bottom of the page in smaller script he wrote: *I am not my own boss. I am not my own master. Master.* When he reread it right away he tried to cross the whole stack of lines out, but the ink was dry or the pen tip disobedient, or maybe he had not the will to press down hard enough.

MR. FEDD had started humming just as the Senior Advisor had fetched their jumpsuits, which meant that he had changed his mind. The Senior Advisor sat back down again, made a pinching, petting motion with his fingers, as though he were petting a spider. Here he was mostly naked before a man from whom did not exactly earn but certainly maintained his salary by nodding *yes* to every word. The dreadfully silent pressures put on a man by such doting made Mr. Fedd regret the invitation, although solitude would have surely been worse, and it was this scale of thoughts that fixed in motion the ticking of thinking that Fedd had successfully avoided since youth.

He could even recall the last time he visited this pocket of his mind. Out the window of the family station wagon young Cole Fedd spotted the president of the family's bank—his father cut the man's hair and was often tipped with cigarillos bearing the bank's logo, and upon smoking them he would ponder in front of young Cole what food must taste like to a man who smokes these damn things every damn day—licking an ice cream cone and walking at the same time. A flurry of staff followed him and formed a rough and moving circle as his stroll quickened and his licks did, too. Cole laughed at the sweating double-suited personage, pressed his tongue to the window and held it there until a curl of fingers found his collar and yanked him face forward accompanied by the following words: "Cole, it ain't easy having everything. It's the hardest thing. If you had everything you'd just about die from exhaustion, though I'm sure right now you expect you'd be in heaven. Everything must go, Cole, before you can be free. It's why I never met a free man all my life." It was the typical jumbled angst of a petty societal cog, and Cole wasn't having any of it. The next day he set out an ice cream vendor like some kids set out lemonade stands, a fine-tuned cooler made from scrap metal, two by fours and filled with plenty of block ice borrowed from the family freezer. He set up shop at the base of Bailing's Investment Bank and awaited the lunch break of the president.

NOW, in the sauna, he saw his young ambitions in all of their perfect naivety. How when his friends had been stirred to exhilaration first by the caught glance of a pretty girl, he had been first stirred to exhilaration when the president himself purchased a cone produced by two shaking hands trying desperately not to spill mom's vanilla down the sides of the stale waffle shell. Now he could recall neither the color of the man's regal suit nor the feeling he had when the president walked close enough to waver like a skyscraper above him, then wink, and then slap him on the back of the head with a whispered, "You're going in the right direction, young-gun," before walking away into the summer sun with a straightforward, frugal gait. His dramatic exit was crippled only by the surety that *yes* young Cole *had* heard a plopping sound down the block, one that signaled without subtlety that the man was one terribly dissatisfied customer. He had rushed after him, scraped the scoop from the cement, and watched it melt in his hands until only a gravelly layer of milk white remained. Waiting for the president to return and cut into him. Tell him his product was trash. Ask for his money back. Cole was under no illusions, and the man's flattery did nothing to wash away the sickly sweet admixture of asphalt and cream that covered his hands.

OVERHEATED now in his sauna, replaying his beginnings, Mr. Fedd watched as he wiped his young hands on the nearest patch of grass, ran home and tried, over the next month, forty-five other recipes, hearing, just before he sampled each, the president's parting words, but then hearing nothing as his tongue touched the ice cream. What Mr. Fedd saw now was a silent film: a satisfied customer melting into the sunset, sugary milk melting around his powerful tongue. *You're going in the right direction, young-gun. Wrong direction, young-gun.* For him that had been the shot that propelled him all the way until the criminal trial. Couldn't it move him again?

But the jury was out, and the verdict public. Somehow, something in him clamored for a retrial.

The red cedar planes were not as pure as years before. Malcolm *had* plugged a few leaks with an insulating caulk, which even when painted to blend seethed out like foam from the mouth of a madman, a madman who had bitten his tongue bloody. Mr. Fedd combed a hand through his hair, and the Senior Advisor whose name was... Mike?... did the same, and this seemingly without consciousness of mimicry. It was hard to have this ape reaching to keep himself on the dole during what was fast becoming one of the most exhausting hours of his life. It was hard to have attendants and papers to sign all the time, an eternal trail of emails and letters and phone calls impossible to answer. It was hard to have everything. Everything except, of course, a hard *no* from the simple tool even now fussing at his wrist with a nervous rhythm across from him, sitting almost symmetrically with his knees open at the same angle as Fedd's, his eyes half-closed, forced lax. He mulled at ways to drag a *no* from the faithful fool, shuddered to even think over the thought required to calculate such an impossible scheme. He reminded himself with his mother's intonation: "You are on vacation. V-A-C-A-T-I-O-N," and let out a long sigh that crossed a border and became a moan.

At least everything was close at hand. But then it wasn't as though he really wanted everything anyhow. That was just the way the three talk show hosts he had met yesterday morning had phrased it: "How does it feel to have everything again, now that all the accusations have been put to sleep?" or "Are you ready to rest now, or get back to business, knowing that you have every-thing again?" or "Everything. You are—you have. Everything." Except, of course, anything that could dignifiedly wear the name of opposition. Flagellation in particular was hard to come by, even at the should-be-willing hands of disgruntled or at least indifferent underlings, and he knew that his faithful employees would sip cyanide or at least take a personal day and hit the shooting range before offending him. And he knew one thing further: that if *he* went loose on *himself* at this chasm of life the raw pleasure of self-applied judgment day would end in a knot of bloodied flesh from which nothing would recover, after which there would be no spirit or even soul left to speak of for the inferno, purgatorio, or paradisio to follow. Punishment. What he really pined after was pain that would begin at a definitive time and end also at a signal to be prearranged between all parties involved. This desire was given an eerie nod by a smirking face opposite him—not the shirtless Senior Advisor sitting arms akimbo, but the face in the knot of wood that snarled with ances-tral sacredness. All of this would require a lawyer. Legal, care-fully-orchestrated suffering. He knew at least twenty by name. He would call them in the morning and at least one would snatch at the job.

> *Suffering*=*redemptive*, *Affliction*=*arbitrary*: *affliction marks*
> *soul with mark of slavery, suffering—pain only physical, taken*
> *by the imagination, but can be transcended by the imagina-*
> *tion. Affliction makes God appear absent for a while.*

This he put down quickly in his journal. She had said some-thing along these lines.

The Senior Advisor stepped judiciously upon insect after insect, his bare feet and palms doing the killing, wiping them on the backside of his legs so Mr. Fedd would not see. Mr. Fedd had seen, and the pathetic sight, which possessed an overwhelming potential to irritate, turned at this moment into a language of utmost loyalty that held his tongue, left him counting the subor-dinates who likewise did sundry little sacrificial things to "keep down the Boss's stress." Although they were not infinite, he could not number them.

The sauna they sat in shook a little under a hard wind, and at once it was like the inside of a narrow train, with two benches that ran along opposite walls, allowing two persons to face one another meditatively, which is what these two did without effort, without wishing to—as if by circumstance and compulsion. Mr. Fedd remembered Her telling him of her favorite novel, *The Idiot* by some Russian author. How the whole thing started with two counterpoint-characters in a train heading to St. Petersburg. Petersburg, built by Peter the Great. Built, rather, by his con-scripted army of serfs, who labored to raise a metropolis amid the Finnish swamps. One character an idiot, *yurodivy*—"a holy fool," she said, "do you know what that is?" she laughed, and he was sure she meant herself as juxtaposed with himself, he who she therefore cast in the part of the ruthless *nouveau riche*.

"Mr. Fedd," said the mostly silent Senior Advisor, "If you don't mind my speaking. You have always been hard on yourself, from the moment I met you. Which is why, by the way, I chose to work for you; having the privilege of choosing, I chose a man who would not be easily blinded by exaggerated perceptions of ordinary virtue. Not that yours are entirely ordinary, but. Oh damn my coffee tongue. Too much again." His voice was sonorous, and Mr. Fedd applauded himself for finding such solid PR material even as he wanted to puncture his own ears.

The Senior Advisor, whose name Cole Fedd conceded was lost beyond recovery, seized a towel and blotted his own neck, wrapped its fuzzed white around his waist, so that Fedd thought at once that previously the Senior Advisor been nude and he had only now covered himself, and increasingly his sweating and intemperately haired legs grew restless and ready to go.

"Do you have a phone, to call Malcolm?" he asked.

"That sound outside. The low rumble. You hear it? Thought it was wind myself, earlier. But that's your sedan. He's been out there keeping it warm for—however long we've been here."

Fedd let his head go lax, let it knock the wall, let the knock resound before saying, "What I'm in need of is a patch of straw, see, a real small patch of it that's maybe even been nibbled at by some animal. What various animals eat straw I don't have the slightest idea, but that would suffice for my bed. And then I'd wake at three am and raise myself to my knees to offer supplications and beg mercy."

"Mr. Fedd, I hate to oppose you, but still. I don't get it. All this noise over your self-incrimination. Really. The case is over and Bobby Wash and his staff are in for it—for what *they* did. Not you. Not you." He almost said openly what they did, paused for a moment, and wheezed rapidly. He had forgotten to breathe. "Why fuss over your innocence? Guilt by association is gone, too, otherwise you'd be in jail with them and not here. Rule of *law,* remember."

"What's your name?"

The Senior Advisor swiveled his head for less than a second, sure that he was alone with the master, that yes the question had been directed at him, and that he should have pinned his name tag to his skin to save the master's face.

"How long have you worked for me? Two years?"

"Seven. Started as a vendor sampler, you know, trekking all over the country with new flavors of ice cream, always trusting the mixture itself, never needing to bluff over the number of cherries per gallon or the smallness of calories. Those days," he said blankly. "Lost a few pounds and one wife since then. She—" but he cut himself off and moved his eyes from Fedd's hairy feet to his well-oiled forehead. The eyes below the lined face possessed a shy sadness, and as Fedd slicked back his wavy black hair with a pocket comb he produced from midair, the Senior Advisor said, "I mean not. I don't want to add to the worries running through your nerves at the moment."

"It's a problem that I didn't know your name. But the bigger problem is the fact that you took no offense. Come on. Take some. Get mad," he said, and felt like a high school theater teacher, unable to coach his actors because he was unable to convince himself.

The Senior Official waited until Mr. Fedd's voice flushed with a faint gleam, his eyes hard on his toes, and only then did he snarf one of the melted truffles the men had brought into the sauna. Of the twenty, Fedd had eaten fifteen, as there were four left. The Senior Official said, disinterestedly, "Oh, no liquor center. What? Butterscotch? So you're really upset. Soberly upset?"

"You should have been there in the courtroom."

"I *was* in the—"

"All their sorry faces looking at me as though they just wanted to eat away at my memory. As if I'm just reveling in memories. Jesus." A newspaper drooped severely beside Fedd, and as he slapped down on it the little black letters transferred to his skin, marking him with the latest story on 'Fat Fedd's Memory on Trial.' The article started with the accusation: Fat Fedd's Memory Cream, *a flavor advertised as a simultaneous memory enhancer, clearly caused amnesia in nine out of ten studied customers. Most did gain a stronger short term memory, but their long term memo-*

ries tended to waste away with every dish or blended shake. The question that consumed fans of Fat Fedd's? Who's to blame? Today, the answer to that question will go down in history, will remain in the memory of ice cream lovers everywhere.

"Where's Malcolm. Do you know?"

"That low rumbling noise outside. He's manning your car. Keeping it warm." He did not use the word *remember* or pull out *I told you once I told you twice.*

"Listen," Mr. Fedd said, and he lunged toward the Senior Advisor, forming his hands into two crescent moons came within inches of closing around the man's neck until he caught himself. "What the hell?" and here Mr. Fedd fell back, balanced on his haunches and shook his head. "I was really looking for you to cut out all nonsense today, to tell me how you never got the raises you wanted, never liked me after all. But you?"

"I actually like you, genuinely, Mr. Fedd. From the heart even, if I can add that."

"Stop it."

The heat made Mr. Fedd's vision oblong, and the room seemed to be sliding, the ascending weariness amazing him. "I think this is our stop," he added, rising, letting the last of the chocolates compete for first place as they pulsed down his choked throat.

MALCOLM did not rise to open the door. He did not move when motioned to. His neck hung long like an ostrich's, his head downward. After a vacuum of seconds that spiraled and spun out and threatened to suck everything in, the Senior Advisor broke the glass and they both smelled the car gas as it escaped hurriedly through the shards. They did not speak. The Senior Advisor plugged his nose and pulled the lever to pop the trunk. He applied a parka first to Mr. Fedd, then to himself. Then he found a tree that seemed to welcome his warm urine as he dialed the emergency number and explained what he could not.

Mr. Fedd fell next to the corpse, still until he could no longer take the albatross hang, the sidelong drooling gaze. He propped Malcolm upright and for a steamy breath believed he heard the thrust of lungs inside the body of the faithful, the only one who knew. He saw his hands form two half-moons and shook the slack valet, first as a father waking his sleepy child, then with hardly-restrained fury, hands around the neck until he birthed the thought that he himself may have killed the blessed old fool. He had to reach between the man's knees to retrieve the newspaper rolled like a scroll there, on his lap. It was the same article he had started to read, and he set himself to finish it quickly, but comprehension came slow. Toward the article's end he came across this:

But the witness who really tipped the scales, according to some discontented opponents, was Malcolm Long, Fedd's valet and confidant. "I suppose the best way to describe the way he treats me is fatherly. Or—I said it wrong. That is, he is like a son to me. He tells me everything. And I know he didn't know those men had put in memory cream that hadn't passed inspection. He wouldn't be able to get away with lying to his own father." Long grinned before the judge, and stepped down from the stand. Of course there is other evidence of Fedd's innocence...

HE had forgotten to turn off the car, but did so carelessly now, as though it did not matter, as though the dizziness did not bother him. He pried at the glove compartment and a pile of postcards poured out. From Her to Cole, from Mozambique. Malcolm. He *had* found them all, then? But he'd—what—*concealed* them from me? *Disobeyed* request that Cole have all to read on vacation? Postcards, not letters tucked in envelopes. Did the old blessed son of a—did he read them? Mr. Fedd felt Malcolm's wrist. He winced. Did *no one* dare disturb him? Was there no one? Was his life *that* vacant? He stared at this father, his once protective eyes only seen as such in this aftermath, in this empty car occupied by no one.

When the Senior Advisor returned they lifted the corpse in unison, although Mr. Fedd had the harder part as there was so much weight in the head. At first they performed this rite like hired professionals from a funeral home, to whom the body was unknown. They laid him in the backseat. He ordered the Senior Advisor away. When he returned a few moments later, he ordered him to put on ice-skates and make circles until told to stop. Cole opened the car door and looked down at the blank line that was Malcom's mouth, the dry cheeks, the dry eyes. He knelt down, spittle shooting out in every direction as he pressed his eyes to Malcolm's, then pulled away to see that the valet had quite literally taken black thread and sewn his mouth shut, from the inside, on the gums. Black stitches, even and unseen on first glance. He pressed his eyes against Malcolm's again, until tears dropped down from his eyes to Malcolm's. Then he rifled recklessly through the sedan, looking for the sewing kit. At last he located it in Malcolm's breast pocket, wrapped in a postcard She had sent from Mozambique.

Affliction in the most awful degree here. The terrible things done to people—this is one thing. But worst is that they need to choose silence or death. There is an affliction so great that it places these souls beyond pity. It pulls from me only horror. Horror.

Cole kicked his heel against the rearview mirror until it came loose, and went with it into the sauna. The strange thing was that he could not find a single inch of thread in the sewing kit.

Trivia. Once, at an intolerable Fatt Fedd's work party, a number of the employees had wanted to play a game of Trivia. He sat there on his phone, making important calls while staying to show them he cared. Then someone said something about spider's silk being stronger than piano wire.

He took a match and struck it, let it cook the edge of the needle until the blue heart of the flame charred the silver, which he then blew until it again reflected light. He took a string of spider silk and slipped it through the needle's eye, then sewed his wrist to the door handle.

"*Judica me,*" he was certain he heard himself say.

Concluding
Unscientific Postscript

IF IT DOESN'T kill you makes you stronger, papa said mama said Adam said that Eve said. In this little room in this little hospice in these last days I am spittle-chin epileptic, host to the horror, the horror, *hostis humani generis* and yet, and yet they hold the holy *hostia* over my body, a circular hole in this inferno. *If it don't kill ye it maketh ye strongeth.* Thus sayeth Quoheleth. In the eyelids the dermis is thinnest, and with closed eyes I still see the shadow of a priest praying psalms over me, thick bellow tone he holds the little black book in his father forgive me hand, extreme unction over my body, over me, the *agnus dei,* the little lamb who made thee, dost thou know who made thee, gave thee life & bid thee feed? He thumbs the fluttery eyelids down now to drown out the doubt drawn in my eyes does he. His hands smell strong of frankincense, of funerary smoke already as though he has just returned from requiem as though he bides his time from one as I lay dying man to another. But fumbling he lets the candles fall like waxen wings of Icarus they form an X across my chest on the wrong side I cannot fly I die. Thumbs the oil on my eyes he hums a Latin *ave* I open them wide to startle him and see only a widening gyre around what might be a smile he prays, *Per istam sanctan unctionem et suam piissimam misericordiam, indulgeat tibi Dominus quidquid per (visum, audtiotum, odorátum, gustum et locutiónem, tactum, gressum deliquisti).*

...

Wake man. This sickness is not unto death.

129

About the Author

JOSHUA HREN teaches and writes at the intersection of political philosophy and literature, and of Christianity and culture. He serves as associate editor of *Dappled Things* and as editor in chief of Wiseblood Books. His scholarly work appears in such journals as *LOGOS*, his poems in such journals as *First Things*, and his short stories in a number of literary magazines. His first academic book, *Middle-earth and the Return of the Common Good: J.R.R. Tolkien and Political Philosophy*, will be published by Cascade Books.